GHOST
OF A
HOPE

Ghost of a Hope
Betty Boo, Ghost Hunter Book Four
© 2012 Beth Dolgner

ISBN-13: 978-0984915682

Published by Redglare Press
Cover by Book Covers by Melody
Print Formatting by The Madd Formatter

BethDolgner.com

Another one for Mom,
my Savannah expert and constant supporter.

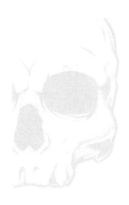

ONE

Pain flared through my hand as my knuckles connected with Maxwell's jaw. He reared back briefly, grunting at the impact, but before I could make another move, he grabbed my arm and spun me around. His hand pressed up against my throat, and he held me tightly, his body solid against my back.

I did the only thing I could think of: I stomped down hard on his foot.

"Ow!" Maxwell released me instantly, his usually handsome face contorted in pain. I was torn between guilt and amusement as he hopped on his uninjured foot.

"I'm sorry," I said, reaching toward him to offer a steadying hand. "I didn't mean to hurt you!"

"Yes, you did." Maxwell managed a small smile. "It's exactly what I told you to do. You've got a lot more power in your feet than you do in your fists. Remember that, Betty, because you might be able to use it to your advantage someday."

I nodded, already heading to the kitchen to grab two bottles of water. I gave one to Maxwell before I plopped down on the couch and drank deeply. I had started to sweat at some point, and even though my hands were wrapped in long strips of cloth, my fingers ached. I unwrapped my right hand and sighed. My knuckles were red and bruised.

"If it makes you feel better, I'm not getting out of this unscathed, either," I said, waggling my fingers.

Maxwell sank down next to me, and one hand came to rest lightly on my thigh. "The only thing that makes me feel better is knowing you'll be able to defend yourself if—"

"When," I interjected.

"When the time comes." Maxwell shuddered. "Teaching you self-defense might have been my idea, but I hate pretending to attack you. It disgusts me."

"I hate fighting back. But you're right; I need all the help I can get."

We fell silent, both of us reluctant to continue the conversation. We knew the demon hunters were going to come after us. We just didn't know how, when, or where. It had been quiet for nearly two weeks, but instead of becoming complacent, we were becoming more wary. Maxwell and I both expected an attack at any moment.

And then there were the nightmares. I had killed a demon hunter, and even though it wasn't the first life I'd taken, it was really hard for me to deal with my guilt. Joseph Stryker had seemed like a nice guy, and I'd even felt attracted to him. I'd kissed him, then stabbed him to death just a couple days later. It weighed heavily on my mind, and the recurring dream of drowning in a sea full of blood woke me up on many nights.

I had killed Joseph to protect Maxwell. It was strange that even though Maxwell was a demon, he was still a better person than Joseph, a man who was willing to hurt innocent people in his zealous passion for banishing demons. Try explaining that to the other hunters, though. Now, Maxwell, our friend Carter, and I were waiting for the inevitable retaliation.

I took a deep breath. I am not worrying about this tonight, I told myself firmly.

"Well, we're not going to worry about any of that tonight," Maxwell said.

"Since when do your demonic abilities include mind-reading? I was just thinking the same thing."

Maxwell looked at me seriously with his pale blue eyes. "Oh, I forgot to tell you. I'm psychic, too. I know everything that goes through that pretty head of yours."

I snorted derisively. "I know that's not true. If it were, you'd be telling me to stop worrying so much. Besides, no supposed psychic has ever convinced me."

"I'll convince you." Maxwell scrunched up his face in mock concentration. "You're thinking that you want to take a shower now so we can get to the restaurant on time."

I glanced at the clock. "No, but it's what I should be thinking. I can't show up at Casbah looking like a prize fighter." I brought my hand up to Maxwell's face and stroked his jaw. "At least you don't have a bruise."

"You don't really punch that hard. My foot, however, is probably bruised. By tomorrow, I'll be healed and you can stomp on me all over again."

One of the perks of being a demon is quick healing time. I'd seen Maxwell recover from a gunshot wound overnight, so I knew that his foot wouldn't hurt anymore by the time dinner was over. I envied that about Maxwell. I'd gotten pretty beat up in the events leading up to Joseph's death. The one week I'd spent on Serenity Island had included brushes with knives, guns, and a hole in the floor. Two weeks later, I still had scabs on my back and a fresh scar on my thigh.

Now I had bruised knuckles, too, and I blamed it all on the demon hunters.

This being at war stuff really sucked.

I leaned over and kissed Maxwell lightly. At least I still had him, though, and I'd face a whole horde of demon hunters to make sure he was safe.

Maxwell looked down at his tee-shirt and jeans. It was the most casual he ever got. "I need a shower, too. See you in half an hour?" I nodded, and after another quick kiss, Maxwell disappeared from my couch. He had materialized home so he could shower there and get dressed for dinner.

Maxwell and I had been together every day for the past two weeks. Now that we knew the demon hunters had us in their sights, Maxwell felt it was safer for both of us if we stayed together. We took turns sleeping at my little apartment or at his historic townhouse, and the only lengthy breaks we got from each other were when I was at work. Even then, Maxwell would occasionally pop up in my office. He'd materialized there on Thursday right behind my boss, who was busy complaining about the temporary receptionist. Luckily, Maxwell pretended he had just walked in the door and that he'd come to take me to lunch.

I had initially had some serious reservations about spending so much time with Maxwell, but it was working out well so far. We were both a little emotionally strained, but it had nothing to do with each other. In fact, I was grateful to have him close to me, both as a protector and as someone who understood my fear.

I was still drying my hair when Maxwell materialized in my bedroom, wearing a deep green three-piece suit. His black hair was perfectly tousled, and his pale jaw still showed no signs of our self-defense training.

I put on a red dress that was several shades darker than my auburn hair. I was already slipping into a pair of black heels when I began to laugh. "You're in green, and I'm in red," I said. "People will think we did this on purpose."

"You look beautiful, so I doubt anyone will care if we're dressed like a couple of presents."

I pulled on my coat, gave my cat Mina a pat on the head, and we left my apartment. Since I live in the historic district in Savannah, Georgia, I'm within walking distance of a lot of places, and Casbah was no exception. Moroccan food was an unusual choice for Christmas Eve, but then, I had unusual friends.

Normally, I would have enjoyed the walk. It was cold out, which was the perfect excuse for snuggling up against Maxwell. As a demon, his skin was always warm, and he kept me toasty on cold nights. The entire historic district was decorated for Christmas, and the pretty squares that dotted the area were all decked out in red bows and long garlands of greenery. I loved strolling the city during December, taking in the festive touches on all the benches, balconies, and doors. On this night, though, we both walked cautiously, our eyes scanning every shadowed doorway and alley that we passed.

And even though we expected it, we were both surprised when someone darted out of a parking garage and grabbed my arm.

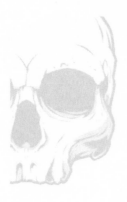

TWO

"Hey!" was all I heard before I balled my hand into a fist. Should I fight, or should I run? Considering the man still had my left arm in his grasp, I ditched the idea of escape. I pulled my free arm back and focused on the man's jaw.

Even as my arm began its arc toward his face, I realized that he was dressed awfully nice for a demon hunter. In fact, he was dressed nicer than anyone I knew, with the exception of one man: Carter Lansford.

But it was too late. Even as my brain commanded my arm to stop moving, my fist hit Carter's face.

Carter dropped my arm but remained silent, his expression shocked, while people all around us gasped and twittered excitedly to each other. I just stood with my hands over my mouth, utterly appalled at what I had just done. Not too long ago, I would have jumped at the chance to punch Carter, but these days we were actually friends.

Maxwell broke the silence, snickering as he said, "Merry Christmas, Carter."

Carter rubbed his jaw absently. "Damn, Betty, I knew you were learning some tricks, but I didn't know you could punch so hard."

"Carter, I am so sorry," I finally said. "So, so sorry. You just startled me, and I panicked."

"It's all right. Good practice for you, I guess." Carter straightened his suit jacket and ran a hand over his waves of blonde hair.

"Afraid I messed up your hair?" I asked. Okay, so Carter and I were friends, but we weren't exactly friendly all the time.

"No, but I'm afraid my face messed up your hand." Carter caught my hand and looked closely. "Your knuckles are a mess."

I snatched my hand away. "Not all of us can afford weekly manicures, Carter."

Instead of retorting, Carter just turned and began to walk with us. The people who had seen the incident realized that there wasn't going to be any drama, and a few tourists actually looked a little disappointed.

Carter was wearing tailored black slacks and a leather jacket that probably cost half of my salary. His family came from old Savannah money, and his dad was a prominent lawyer. Those things explained the nice clothes but didn't excuse Carter's snobbery. He was, at least, getting better. Either that, or I was getting used to him.

"I'm sorry," I said again.

Carter shrugged languidly. I didn't think he was going to respond further, but after a moment he spoke quietly. "I nearly tackled my mailman last week. He came up to the door to drop off a package, and when I heard him, I thought for sure it was a hunter."

"I still don't like you staying by yourself. Can't your parents put you up for a while?"

"What am I supposed to tell them? That I got caught up with a demon and his girlfriend, was held at gunpoint, had to escape a bunch of demon hunters who wanted to kill me, and am now looking over my shoulder every two minutes?"

"Tell them your townhouse is being treated for termites," Maxwell suggested.

Carter's only response was a quiet "humph." I thought he was just annoyed, but when I glanced at him, I could see the worry creasing his usually smooth forehead.

The three of us arrived at the restaurant on the heels of my best friend Daisy and her husband Shaun. Daisy was two months pregnant, and so far pregnancy really agreed with her. She was more bubbly than ever, and her face glowed. When she saw us, Daisy immediately turned and opened her arms. I expected her to hug me and was surprised when she embraced Carter instead. "Happy Christmas Eve!" she said.

Carter mumbled something in response before Daisy gave the same treatment to Maxwell and me. Although she and Shaun were well aware of the danger that the rest of us were in, Daisy's optimism was impossible to overcome. I was grateful for it: on days when I felt overwhelmed, a phone call to Daisy always made me feel better.

We were shown to low cushions arranged around a small table. Moroccan music played quietly in the background, and soon I had a cup of hot tea in front of me.

After we ordered, Carter told Daisy about my "attack." He expected sympathy, but instead Daisy just laughed until tears ran down her face. "I would have paid to see that," she said when she finally recovered enough to speak.

Carter shook his head. "I should have known better. I've been attacked by both of the women at this table."

Daisy tried to look shocked, but she was smiling too much. "What will it take for you to finally forget about that little incident on the stairs?"

"A case. I haven't investigated since I got home, and a ghost or two would be a nice distraction."

"It's always quiet around Christmas," Shaun said.

"Families are too busy with the holidays to notice any ghosts."

"Cheer up, Carter," I said. "Maybe the Ghost of Christmas Past will visit you tonight to show you all the bad things you've done." I was teasing Carter, but I could use a paranormal investigation, too. I hadn't been out with The Savannah Spirit Seekers—my ghost hunting team—in over a month. We just hadn't been getting any calls from people who needed help, and then I'd gone to Serenity Island with Carter for two weeks.

Thinking about The Seekers was the only sad moment I had during dinner. Daisy and Shaun were Seekers, too, but we were missing Lou. He had been our tech genius and one of the nicest people I knew. At least, until he had become a demon hunter. Now he was one of the hunters who had declared war on Maxwell, Carter, and me. It wasn't so much that I missed having him in The Seekers as I just missed having him as my friend.

None of us could have guessed that Carter would fill the vacant spot Lou left in The Seekers. He wasn't an official member, and I doubted he ever would be, even if we offered it to him. Carter had his own team—The East Coast Paranormal Authorities—and he would never agree to be a part of someone else's group. Still, he and I had been through a lot together lately, and it just didn't feel right to exclude him from our group's Christmas Eve dinner.

I only took two bites of my dessert before I put down my fork, leaned back against the cushions, and declared myself absolutely stuffed. Several belly dancers were shimmying their way through the restaurant, and I watched them lazily while Maxwell and Carter debated who was the best men's tailor in Savannah.

I heard my phone ringing inside my purse, and I pulled it out just to check the caller I.D. I was sure it was only someone calling to wish me a Merry Christmas. The number was local, but I didn't recognize it, so I ignored the call.

By the time the same person had called back three times in five minutes, I was getting dirty looks from other diners near us. I clambered up from the cushions and answered the phone as I walked outside.

"Oh, thank goodness," a female voice said.

"Can I help you?"

"I sure hope so. I've got a nasty ghost here, and someone needs to come take care of it."

"When you say 'nasty,' what exactly do you mean?" I asked.

"I mean it's causing all kinds of problems for my band."

"You're in a band?"

"No." The woman paused, then laughed self-consciously. "I should have started by saying that I'm Annie. I own The Hex."

Now things were making more sense. The Hex was a small bar and music venue on West Congress. "I'm sure we can come in after Christmas. We don't have any other investigations booked right now," I said.

"Well," Annie hesitated, and she sounded sheepish when she continued. "I was hoping you could come over tonight, just to talk to the band. They're playing our Christmas Eve show, and they're leaving town as soon as they pack up tonight. They've experienced the worst of it."

I considered briefly. We were done with dinner, and I knew Maxwell wouldn't mind walking over to The Hex before we headed home. "All right. I can be there in about half an hour."

Annie thanked me a few times before hanging up. When I got back to our table inside the restaurant, I reached down and ruffled Carter's hair. "Looks like the Ghost of Christmas Past is hanging out at The Hex."

Carter just grumbled and began meticulously rearranging his hair, but Shaun pried me for details. When I was done, the only person who didn't look excited was Daisy. "How did she get your cell phone number?" she asked. "The number listed on our website is your home phone."

"I don't know. It's Savannah, so maybe someone who knows me passed it on. It's kind of a small world in the historic district." Besides, I added silently, all that really mattered was that we had a case, and that felt really good.

Daisy and Shaun declined going to The Hex with us since they were immediately hitting the road to visit Shaun's parents for Christmas. The drive was only a few hours and they would arrive well before midnight, but they were anxious to get it over with. I hugged Daisy and Shaun on the sidewalk and insisted that they call when they got in. "And have a Merry Christmas," I added.

"You, too. Enjoy your first Christmas with Maxwell." I could practically feel Daisy's curiosity about what Maxwell might have gotten me for Christmas, and I knew she'd be calling me early the next morning to inquire.

Carter insisted on driving Maxwell and me to The Hex, even though it would have been a short walk. He figured the fewer dark alleys we had to walk past, the better.

Loud music blared from the front door of The Hex, but before we could go in, a tall, thin woman with long purple hair hailed us. She had a row of big hoops in each ear, and tattoos covered her arms. Her black dress, though, was simple and elegant.

"I'm Annie," the woman said. "Thank you so much for coming."

I shook Annie's hand and assured her that we'd do our

best to help. Before I could ask how she'd gotten my phone number, Annie continued. "The band doesn't go on until ten, so you have some time to talk to them. I just don't understand what's going on. Our ghost is usually pretty quiet."

"You've had paranormal activity here for a while?" I asked.

"Since we moved into the building. But it's the usual stuff, you know? Things getting moved, footsteps, that feeling that you're not alone." Annie waved dismissively, taking the same attitude most Savannah residents had of the city's abundant paranormal population. "Today, though, has been crazy, and most of the activity has been on stage or in the green room right behind it. Come on."

The music blaring from the speakers inside was heavy and dark, and dim light radiated from chandeliers. Almost every surface in the place was painted black, so I wasn't surprised to see it was the wardrobe color of choice for nearly everyone packed onto the floor.

Annie deftly skirted the crowd and led us to a room behind the stage. I knew that Maxwell, Carter, and I stuck out conspicuously, and I was glad to slip into the room.

Four guys about my age were staring at us. One of them, who had long brown hair, said, "You should have gotten here two minutes ago."

"Why? What happened?" I launched right into investigator mode and forgot to even introduce myself.

"This happened." One of the others, who had short blonde hair and big turquoise earrings, held out his leg. He was wearing shorts despite the cold weather, and his shin was bleeding. He pointed at a pile of broken glass, which sat in a puddle of water. "The glass was hurled off the table, and one of the shards got me."

"Maybe it just slid off the table on its own," Carter said. His tone was condescending, and he zipped up his jacket, as if he wanted more of a barrier between himself and these other guys. "When condensation builds up under a glass, it can make the glass slide across the table top. It might have slid right off the edge."

The blonde guy was already shaking his head. "Nope. It *flew*. That glass was thrown to the ground; it didn't just fall."

Annie spoke up then, saying, "Do you need to go get stitches?"

"Nah. I'll be all right. It's metal."

"You said it was glass," I corrected.

"No, heavy metal."

If I had felt conspicuous before, then I was sure that I had a neon sign above my head now, telling everyone that I didn't fit in here. "You're in a metal band," I concluded.

The blonde one leaned over and extended his hand. "Yep. Obsidian Sky. I'm Tim, that's Dillan, Mo, and Khalifa."

"Did you bring this ghost with you?" It was the first time Maxwell had spoken since we came in. His voice was quiet, but I could see every back in the room straighten as everyone really looked at him for the first time. Annie looked like she wanted to ask him out right then and there, but the band looked unnerved. Maxwell had a commanding presence when he wanted to, and I wondered if that was because of his personality or because he was a demon. Either way, four heads shook in response.

"Nothing like this has happened to us before," the one with long hair spoke up again. Dillan, I remembered. "It started when we were loading in. We'd put stuff on the stage only to find it pushed onto the floor when we came back."

"And then I got pushed onto the floor." One of the guys held up a bandaged wrist and hand.

"We know you just tripped, Khalifa. Stop blaming it on

13

the ghost." The skinniest of the band members had said that, and he was nervously twirling a drumstick in his fingers.

Khalifa opened his mouth to retort, but I jumped in. "Are those spoons sticking out of your bandage?"

"I think I broke my wrist when I fell, and I needed a splint. It's going to be tough to play tonight."

"Why didn't you go to the hospital?"

Khalifa shrugged. "I'll go later. After Christmas, maybe."

I wanted to argue, but I wasn't one to talk. After all, a bullet had grazed my thigh, and I'd let an amateur stitch up the wound. Instead of going to a doctor once I got home, I had simply kept my bandages fresh and eventually let Maxwell take out the stitches.

I was so totally metal.

I sat down in a vacant chair and pointed at Mo. "And what's happened to you?"

"The ghost seems to like my drums. We did our sound check, then came back here, and we kept hearing noises, like a kid banging on my drum set. Every time we'd check, though, there was nobody there."

I nodded. "Not everyone has been getting violently attacked. That's good. What else has happened today?"

The four band mates looked at each other, and I could tell they were having some sort of silent conversation. Even Annie looked uncomfortable as she shifted her gaze to the ceiling.

After a long pause, Dillan finally spoke up. "My hair got lit on fire." He turned around, and I could see the uneven edges of his hair where bits had burned off. I had a horrible sense of déjà vu.

"Oh, Betty, do you think it's back?" Carter sounded as shaken as I felt.

"I don't think it works that way," I said hesitantly, glancing at Maxwell.

Maxwell was shaking his head. "No, it's not demonic. I know what you're thinking, but this is just a ghost we're dealing with here."

"How do you know?" Khalifa spoke up. "Someone else already said it sounded like demonic stuff going on."

Maxwell looked intently at Khalifa. "I know. Trust me."

"He's an expert," Carter supplied.

"One of those demonologists?" Tim asked. He was tying a ripped-up tee-shirt around his leg, ignoring the blood that had dripped down into his shoe.

"Demon something-or-other," Carter answered, his face deadpan.

I snickered, then covered my mouth until I could put on an appropriately serious face. A violent ghost wasn't good, and I didn't like knowing that people were getting hurt. A cut leg and a broken wrist were nothing to laugh at, but I felt immense relief knowing we weren't dealing with a demonic entity. The last time I'd dealt with one, my hair had been lit on fire, and that's why I sported a short, jaw-length hairstyle now. Just looking at Dillan's burned hair brought back vivid memories of the charred smell and the fear of that night.

When I recovered from my laughter, I addressed Dillan. "How did the ghost light your hair on fire?" I knew that demons could summon fire, but I'd never heard of a ghost doing it.

Dillan looked a little embarrassed. "I meditate before every show, and I bring candles for it. My eyes were closed, and suddenly I smelled smoke. The ghost had pushed one of the candles closer to me, and my hair got too close to the flame."

I nodded sympathetically. "I can relate, believe me. Anything else we should know about?"

The four band mates looked at each other, then at me. "That's it," Mo said.

Carter turned to Annie. "We'll want to hear some more details about your experiences with the ghost, but we can do that later. Betty will do some research into the history of the building, too." I was amused at Carter's take-charge attitude. Clearly, although Annie had called The Seekers for help, Carter had every intention of investigating with us.

"We've got the history taken care of. I'll e-mail a copy of our info over to you," Annie promised. "Now, when can you come back?"

"I'm off work for the next week, so anything works for me," I said.

"The sooner the better. We have a New Year's Eve show here, and I'd hate for those bands to have trouble, too."

We agreed to return the day after Christmas. Daisy and Shaun would be home by then, though I knew Daisy would have to sit out this investigation: it was dangerous enough for all of us, let alone for a pregnant woman.

I rose to leave, but Khalifa stopped me. "Wait, what if something else happens tonight?"

This was one of the worst parts of being a ghost hunter. They needed immediate help, but there was little we could do with a roomful of people waiting for the show. I never wanted to tell a client that they would just have to deal with it, especially if it was a violent haunting.

"You can say a prayer for protection. You can also use salt: make a ring of it around this room and around the stage. As you do, envision it keeping out anything evil or harmful." I paused, seeing the skepticism on the faces before me. "Most importantly, don't be afraid. Fear can open you up to even more bad stuff."

"You're afraid," a deep, raspy voice said in my ear.

I jumped and turned around, but only Carter stood there, a few feet away from me. "Did you hear that?" I asked.

Carter looked closely at me. "No, but you're bleeding."

THREE

I followed Carter's gaze and saw that a wide patch on my dress was an even darker red than the rest of the material. It was on my thigh, over my gunshot wound. I touched the spot gingerly, and my fingers came away red.

Throwing modesty aside, I hiked up my dress and saw that my scar had opened up again. "How did that happen? It was healed!" I hadn't even felt any pain, either. On closer inspection, I saw that only part of the cut had reopened, but it was bleeding enough that Annie turned her head away.

Maxwell found some napkins lying on a table and pressed them against my leg. His expression was worried. "What did you hear?"

When I described the voice I'd heard, Annie didn't seem at all surprised. "That sounds like Mort, our ghost. He's spoken to people before, and they always say he's got a deep voice, and he talks in a loud whisper. But he's never caused problems, and I don't know why he'd be doing all of this."

"Maybe he's not," I said. "It could be another ghost who has taken up residence here. We'll try to find some answers for you when we investigate."

Annie gestured at my leg, though she continued to avert her eyes. "I'm sorry you got hurt."

I kept my voice casual, even though I was a little shaken. "Don't blame the ghost. I got hurt a couple weeks ago, and it looks like the cut reopened. The timing is just a coincidence, I'm sure." But I wasn't sure, and I was not looking forward to the investigation. Facing a violent ghost wasn't the kind of case I'd been hoping for.

We said our goodbyes and left the green room, and as I passed the stage, the same disembodied voice spoke in my ear. All he said was, "Betty."

Despite my wound, I hustled out of The Hex and didn't speak until we were in Carter's car, driving toward my apartment.

"I just don't like it," I was saying as Carter's Mercedes came to a stop in the alley behind my apartment. "It knew my name, and seeing that guy's hair burned was too similar to what happened at Sam MacIntosh's house. Even if it's a ghost and not a demon, it still felt like a warning."

"We'll get some answers the day after tomorrow," Carter assured me. He was always so confident that he'd do one investigation and get all the answers in one night. "In the meantime, Merry Christmas."

I leaned up from the backseat and gave Carter a makeshift hug. "Merry Christmas, Carter."

Soon Maxwell and I were alone in my apartment. It's on the ground floor of a converted carriage house from the 1800s, and the brick walls did little to keep out the cold. I cranked up the heat before slipping into pajamas.

"Demon hunters, a violent ghost...what else are we going to have to deal with?" I asked as I slid into bed next to Maxwell. I curled up against his bare skin, loving the heat radiating off of him.

"I'd say you could turn down this investigation, but I know you better than that. You want to help, and you feel obligated to help."

I nodded against Maxwell's chest.

"We'll deal with everything. You've overcome worse." Maxwell's voice was low but confident. "Remember, you're not supposed to worry about anything until after Christmas."

I brought my hand up to my head and mimicked turning a key. "My brain is officially turned off."

"Oh, no, here I'd hoped to turn you on." Maxwell turned my face to his and kissed me deeply. I felt his hand slide under my shirt, and he pulled me close against him. I angled my leg to keep my newly-bandaged thigh from getting bumped, but I pushed closer to him with every other body part.

I should have known better than to put on pajamas in the first place. They wound up being thrown on the floor.

When I woke up in the morning, Maxwell was sprawled on his stomach, still naked, on top of the covers. One arm was draped over me, but I was snuggled deep under the comforter. I could feel my cat Mina's little body curled up at my feet. The sun angled in through my blinds, and I knew we had slept past our normal hour. I sighed and lay there for a few minutes without moving. It was a perfect moment, and not a single demon hunter entered my thoughts. Why can't every day start like this? I thought. It was so peaceful.

There was a deep blast as a cargo ship coming up the Savannah River sounded its horn. Even though I was blocks away from the river, the sound was still booming. Maxwell stirred next to me, and he cracked one eye open. "Merry Christmas," he said.

"Merry Christmas. And Merry Christmas to you, Lieutenant Griffin!" My living room blinds banged in response as Lieutenant Ambrose Griffin—the Confederate ghost who served as a sort of security guard at my apartment—greeted me in response.

"I'd give you your present now, but I'm guessing you want coffee first," Maxwell continued.

I nodded as I slid the covers off of me. I needed my coffee fix before my brain would be awake enough for presents.

I peeked out the kitchen window while the coffee brewed and saw tourists already walking past. Savannah was a popular destination at this time of year, especially for people who were trying to escape snow and ice.

Maxwell soon joined me, wearing jeans and a black tee-shirt that I knew he hadn't brought with him. "I didn't even hear you leave," I said.

Maxwell kissed me on top of my head. "Because you haven't had any coffee yet."

By the time I'd gotten through half a cup, I was impatient to give Maxwell his present. It hadn't been easy finding something for him: after spending hundreds of years on Earth, Maxwell has pretty much owned everything worth owning. I had briefly considered giving Maxwell a copy of Carter's book, just because I knew it was something he definitely did not have already. I had decided against it about half a second after the thought entered my mind.

Instead, I pulled a small gift-wrapped box out from underneath my tiny, three-foot tall Christmas tree and handed it to Maxwell. He pulled me down onto the couch next to him and unwrapped it. "A pocket watch? Betty, it's beautiful."

"Look at the inscription on the back," I told him.

Maxwell read the words aloud. "To my darling. Savannah, Georgia, 1893."

"You lived here then, in the house that Faith haunts." Faith was the ghost of a little girl, and she had helped me find Maxwell after another demon took him captive. Faith had already been a ghost when Maxwell moved into the house, and he had looked at her as a sort of daughter.

Maxwell looked up at me. "This is perfect." He leaned forward and kissed me, then drew me into a tight embrace. "Thank you."

I was surprised at how relieved I felt that Maxwell liked it until I realized that it was the first gift I had ever given him. It was also our first Christmas together (the first of many, I hoped), and I didn't want to look back on this day with regret because I chose the wrong present.

Maxwell eventually released me and retrieved a box from his jacket pocket. It was even smaller than the box that had contained his pocket watch. Maxwell started to hand it to me, then drew it back. "It's not an engagement ring," he said, one corner of his mouth turned up.

"Well, I should hope not. We haven't been dating that long. But why are you telling me this?"

"Because you thought it. You looked really excited, and then you looked really nervous."

"You've seen that look a lot, have you?" I asked sarcastically. I raised my hands. "No, don't tell me. I don't want to know."

Maxwell placed the box in my hands. "I have never been married. If I ever ask you, you'll be the first."

I knew I was blushing, so I concentrated on opening the box. Inside was a sapphire ring, clearly a vintage one. The gem was in a delicate filigree setting. "Oh, Maxwell," was all I could say.

"It's the birthstone for September, the month we met," Maxwell said as he took the ring from its box. "It is also supposed to help with spiritual enlightenment, clairvoyance, and healing."

"And it's absolutely beautiful." Maxwell solemnly slid

the ring onto my finger. It fit perfectly. "It's blue, like your eyes," I said.

I was admiring the ring when Maxwell caught my hand and kissed each of my fingertips. He placed my hand over his heart and looked at me earnestly. "I've never celebrated Christmas before," he said.

"Why not? Oh, I guess it's not exactly a demon's favorite holiday."

"No. But you've gotten me to do a lot of things that I normally wouldn't." Maxwell was still gazing at me, and I wondered if he was trying to convey more than he was saying.

"Is that a bad thing?"

"No, just different." Maxwell paused, and I could tell he was trying to choose his next words. "For the first time in my existence, I've actually begun to feel remorse for some of the things I've done. I always used to be so proud of the lives I'd ruined, the souls I'd sent to hell. Some of those people deserved it. Others...maybe it was unfair of me to target them."

Maxwell's whole purpose on Earth was to spread fear and chaos, and to ultimately win more souls for hell by making people lose their faith in God. When we had met, Maxwell had spoken of some of his conquests with pride, like a football player would brag about winning a game. I had accepted it as part of who he was, and, frankly, I just tried not to think about it. As long as Maxwell was good to me, I figured that was all that mattered. And if he was busy being good to me, then that meant he wasn't out ruining someone else's life.

Hearing a demon—even *my* demon—admit to feeling remorse was stunning. "You shouldn't feel guilty," I said carefully. "You had no choice. It was your job."

Maxwell still held my hand against his heart, and he absent-mindedly rubbed the back of my hand with his thumb as he spoke. "I had a choice in who I targeted, though. I took a lot of joy in destroying the really good people, the ones who thought their faith was unshakable. Destroying one person's life often set off a chain reaction that negatively affected a lot of others, too. I see some of that in what I've done to your life, even though I've always tried to help you. If it weren't for me, you wouldn't be living in fear of demon hunters. Lou would still be your friend. You wouldn't have blood on your hands."

I looked at Maxwell seriously, but my tone was teasing. "Are you breaking up with me again?"

"No. I know better than to do that again. I'm just saying that you're turning me into...a better man isn't quite the right term...a worse demon. What's amazing is that I don't mind it at all. In fact, I kind of like it."

I took Maxwell's free hand with my own and gave it a squeeze. "I love you," I said.

"I love you, too, Betty." Maxwell leaned in and kissed me, and I felt him smile as he pulled away just enough to say, "I'm glad I got to celebrate my first Christmas with you."

———

I felt like Christmas was my one day of calm before the approaching storm. I didn't have a good feeling about the investigation at The Hex. I shared my concerns with my mom when Maxwell and I went to her house on Savannah's Southside for Christmas dinner. Her response was a crisp, "Well, whatever happens, I'm sure you've been through worse." She eyed Maxwell as she spoke. When Maxwell had broken up with me in an attempt to keep me safe from demon hunters (or even other demons), I had simply told Mom that Maxwell had suddenly stopped calling me. She wasn't happy that I'd "taken him back."

24

Even Mom's aversion to Maxwell couldn't ruin my Christmas, but I woke up the next morning feeling like there was a heavy weight on my heart. The sky was overcast and ominous, the perfect complement to my mood.

We had spent the night at Maxwell's, and the only thing I had accomplished during daylight hours was going over the history of The Hex. Annie had emailed me copies of their research, but I found nothing that could explain a violent haunting.

When seven o'clock arrived, I pulled on a black Seekers tee and grabbed my "paranormal pack," as Daisy called it, with all of my equipment. Daisy had not been happy about missing out on the investigation, and she had made me promise to text her with updates every hour.

Maxwell was sitting at the small table in his expansive kitchen, typing on his laptop. "I'm heading out. Wish me luck," I said, leaning down to his level.

Maxwell waited until I had kissed him good-bye before he said, "I'm going with you." At my surprised expression, he continued. "One, you're dealing with a dangerous ghost, and two, you staying out until the early hours of the morning doesn't worry me as much as you coming home alone in the early hours of the morning. Between the ghost and the hunters, it's too dangerous for you to go alone."

I wasn't going to argue. The more reinforcements I had tonight, the better.

Shaun and Carter were already at The Hex when I arrived. The bar had closed for the night just so we could investigate, and the trio of college students who tried to follow me through the front door grumbled when Annie turned them away.

The overhead lights were on, though the black walls kept the place from being too bright. Annie led us to the office, where Shaun was setting up two video monitors on top of a desk. "Has anything else happened?" I asked Annie.

"Sort of. One of my bartenders was cleaning up after our Christmas Eve show. She leaned down to put some things under the bar, and when she stood up, she smelled something burning. There was a lit cigarette lying on the bar right in front of her, and her hair had gotten scorched."

"It's an interesting coincidence, but it doesn't sound paranormal," I said.

Annie paused and faced me. "There were only three of us here at the time. None of us smoke, and that cigarette had just been lit."

"Oh." Maybe our ghost was a pyromaniac.

"Hey, Boo," Carter said, coming into the office behind us. He was tucking his phone into his pocket, so I knew he'd been on a call instead of helping Shaun. Typical Carter.

"Shaun, do you want me to get the infrared cameras set up?" I asked, ignoring Carter.

"Already done. I got here early." Shaun lowered his voice and leaned toward me, but he whispered so loudly that everyone heard him as he said, "Daisy was nagging me with all kinds of ghost safety advice. I figured I was better off here." Even as he spoke, Shaun's phone began to ring. He smirked and held it up so we could see Daisy's name on the caller I.D.

Shaun had set up two infrared cameras: one pointing at the stage and another in the green room, facing the table that the glass had been sitting on before something had thrown it.

Annie gave us the key to The Hex and left, but not until after Carter reassured her a few times. She was afraid for us, nervous about leaving her bar in our hands, and anxious to get some answers. Carter was good at smooth-talking clients. And ghosts, for that matter. I hoped he would be able to smooth-talk our ghost into crossing over, or at least into being a kinder, gentler spirit in the future.

"Let's get started," I said when Carter returned from escorting Annie out.

"You and I are partners," Carter said immediately. "Sorry, Maxwell. Betty and I are a good pair. Plus, I'm afraid that if you two team up, you may not get much in the way of results. You might be too over-protective of her."

"That's exactly why I'm here," Maxwell said, "but you do have a point. If it gets dangerous, we'll rethink our pairings."

"What," Shaun spoke up, "no one wants to be my partner?"

"We're too used to Daisy being your partner," I said. "We'll make it up to you: you and Maxwell can take the first shift."

Carter and I settled into office chairs to watch the video monitors while Maxwell and Shaun went to the green room. Maxwell had never actually been on an investigation, but he had the ability to communicate with ghosts, so he would probably be an asset to us. On the green room monitor, we saw Shaun put down his tape recorder to have an EVP session. I sure hoped he was capturing something on the recorder, but I could tell by both his and Maxwell's body language that nothing was happening. After half an hour, they moved to the stage, but they came up empty-handed again.

It was time for Carter and me to try to make contact with the ghost. I still had that heavy feeling in my chest, and I took a deep breath in an effort to relax. Like I had told the band, going in scared could cause trouble, and I knew that this ghost had plenty of that to offer.

Carter and I sat down on the floor of the green room. I

pulled out my camera as Carter put his tape recorder on the floor in front of us, and we turned off our flashlights in tandem. With no windows, it was utterly dark in the room.

"My name is Carter," he began, and I followed with, "and my name is Betty. We want to communicate with you."

There were several loud scraping sounds from every corner of the room, and I instinctively brought my arms up to cover my face and head.

It was a good thing I did.

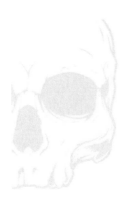

FOUR

Even amid the noise, I noticed the smell of stale beer. Something hard hit my arm, and then a larger object slammed into my back. I was sitting cross-legged, or I probably would have fallen forward. A couple more objects hit me, but they were so light that I barely felt them.

The room returned to absolute silence after that, but I kept my eyes squeezed shut and my arms over my head. I heard Carter swearing next to me. "You okay?" he asked.

"I think so. You?"

"I'm fine, but it sounded like stuff was flying across the room."

"It was," I said.

"How could you see it in the dark?"

"I didn't see anything. It all landed on me." I finally lifted my head and felt for my flashlight. When I turned it on, I saw that there was a pile of stuff around me. A beer bottle lay at my feet, and fortunately it hadn't broken when it hit my arm. Behind me, a lamp sat on its side, the light bulb shattered. A number of plastic cups were scattered around me, too, and I figured they had been the softer objects hurled at me.

Maxwell burst into the room at that moment, but he stopped short when he saw the shattered glass. "I'm fine," I said before he could even speak, "but I could use a hand getting up."

Maxwell stepped gingerly around the broken glass and pulled me to my feet. His hands were shaking. "It looked awful on the video monitor," he said.

"It sounded awful in here," Carter agreed. "That was crazy."

"Is Shaun alone?" I said. "I'm not sure that's a good idea."

"I think everyone should come back to the office." Maxwell hesitated, then shook his head. "I was so scared that I didn't even think to materialize into the room with you. Not that it would have made a difference."

"Carter, did you get hurt?" We began walking back to the office, and I could see that Carter was rubbing his arm.

"No, I'm fine. The ghost threw everything at you. I got a weird tingle on my arm while that was going on, though. You know that feeling you get when someone invades your personal space? It was like that. I felt like someone came and sat down between us, except there really wasn't enough room for another body."

I was considering what that might mean when we reached the office. Shaun launched out of his chair and grabbed my arms. "Are you all right?"

"I will be if you stop squeezing me. You're having a very Daisy reaction."

"She knows something happened. When we saw everything hit you, Maxwell took off at the same time that Daisy texted me. She wanted to know if you were okay."

I could only smile at Daisy's instincts. She has always been the most intuitive person in The Seekers. Apparently, she could get flashes of insight even from miles away.

Shaun was clearly waiting for me to answer him, even though I'd already assured him that I was fine. "Tell her

I'm perfectly all right, just a little shaken." Shaun nodded and immediately began typing on his phone.

I sat down in a chair, chewing my lip as I thought. "What are we dealing with here? We thought it was a violent ghost, but maybe not. The injuries to the band members could have been a coincidence: maybe the ghost didn't mean for anyone to actually fall off the stage or for the glass to cut anyone. Maybe it's lashing out for attention, not to cause harm."

"You forget that the ghost also likes setting hair on fire. That's not an accident," Carter said.

"But I didn't actually get hurt in that room," I countered.

"Maybe the ghost wants to get a message across. Something that has to do with fire." Shaun looked thoughtful, too, now that he had assured his wife of my safety.

"Maxwell, are you getting any insight?" I had hoped that Maxwell might be able to clear all of this up just by having a conversation with the ghost.

"Not a thing. I can tell there's a spirit here, but it seems like wherever I go, it moves away. I think it knows what I am, and it wants nothing to do with me. That happens sometimes." Maxwell gave me a wink. "I promise I'm not taking it personally."

"Maybe there are two spirits here, and one of them feels threatened by the other." I sat up straighter as the theory began to take shape in my head. "Annie said that The Hex came with a resident ghost. Just one. But in the green room, Carter felt something sit between us when all that stuff was thrown across the room. Maybe a new ghost has taken up residence, and the old ghost is trying to get rid of him."

"You think that those things were thrown at another ghost, not at you," Carter said.

"Exactly."

"Only one way to find out. Shall we go sit on the stage?" Carter extended his hand and helped me up. I wanted to say no, and part of me hoped that Maxwell would intervene, but no one protested. Instead, Shaun and Maxwell simply urged caution, and Maxwell promised to materialize by my side if anything happened.

Carter and I sat down in the center of the stage—no way was I going to get close to the edge and risk getting pushed over. As I settled in, I closed my eyes and said a brief but fervent prayer for protection. I even prayed for Carter.

The bar was less dark than the green room, thanks to windows along the outer wall. The noise of cars and people outside drifted in. I felt safer than I had in the green room, less disconnected from the rest of the world.

Carter placed his tape recorder in front of us again, and after we said our names, I braced myself for another incident. When nothing happened, I began to relax. "What was your name?" I asked. "How many of you are here with us? Why did you push that guy off the stage?" I paused between each question, hoping that we would hear an answer when we played the recording later.

"Why did you throw things at Betty?" Carter added. "Are you angry?"

We sat silently for a time, and I took a number of pictures with my camera. Still, nothing happened.

Carter decided to try a different approach. "Are you upset that we're here? Do you want us to leave?"

My left shoulder felt cold suddenly, like I was sitting under an air-conditioning vent. The same low, raspy voice I had heard on Christmas Eve spoke in my ear again. "Yes."

I gasped. "It just said, 'yes.'"

"Are you sure? I didn't hear anything." I couldn't see Carter's frown, but I could hear it.

"It whispered in my ear."

Now Carter addressed the ghost. "If you just spoke to Betty, do it again so we'll know you mean it."

The voice spoke again, louder this time. "Get out, Betty."

I immediately stood up and turned on my flashlight. "He means it. Let's go." I raised my voice. "We're going, okay? Just give us a little time to pack up our equipment."

Carter grabbed his tape recorder and followed me back to the office. "We're leaving," I announced. When I described what I had heard, no one argued with me, except Carter.

"Maybe he just wants you to leave, since he called you by name," he said. "The rest of us could stay to investigate more."

"No, I think we should all go," said Maxwell. "It seems like the activity is centered around Betty tonight, so I doubt you'd get any results without her here. Plus, I don't like the idea of us splitting up."

"Yeah, Carter," I said, poking his arm. "That's how somebody winds up dead in every horror movie."

We packed up quickly, though I did find a broom to sweep up the shattered light bulb in the green room before we left. We would certainly have an interesting story to relate to Annie, but I was disappointed that we hadn't gotten any answers for her. I hoped the video and tape recordings might turn up something we had missed.

We were all disappointed when we parted for the night. (All except Daisy, who called to express her delight that we were done and all still in one piece.) It had been a scary and frustrating night. I lay awake for a long time that night, thinking about the strange activity and wondering what it meant.

The following day was Tuesday. It felt odd not having to be at work. I had taken two weeks off when Carter and I went to Serenity Island, even though we wound up being there for only a week, and now the office where I worked was closed for the week between Christmas and New Year's. I hardly knew what to do with so much free time.

Carter reviewed the EVP sessions on his tape recorder and called to report that he didn't find a thing, not even the phantom voice that had whispered in my ear. My photos didn't turn up anything, either. All we had to show for the night was video of our incident in the green room and a bunch of broken glass in a trashcan.

I was feeling pretty down about the whole thing, and worrying about the haunting at The Hex only compounded my worry about the demon hunters. We were at Maxwell's house again, and after lunch, I sat on the couch, staring out the bay window overlooking the street and wondering if everyone who walked past was secretly spying on us for the hunters.

After an hour of that, Maxwell leaned over the back of the couch and rested his chin on the top of my head. His fingers massaged my shoulders, and I closed my eyes. "I feel like I'm going to crack," I said.

"I know. Which is why we're going somewhere that no demon hunter or ghost can follow." Maxwell refused to say more, but it didn't keep me from asking for clues as we drove out of Savannah.

I was really mystified when Maxwell pulled into the airport. "I haven't packed a bag, so I know we're not going on vacation," I said.

"No, we're just spending the afternoon in the air." Maxwell bypassed the main terminal of the airport, where commercial flights arrive and depart, and instead drove to a small building some distance away.

When we walked inside, a man wearing khakis and a polo shirt greeted Maxwell warmly. "Good to see you again, Mr. Damon. And you must be the charming Betty Boorman," he said, turning to me. "I'm Nick, and I'm at your service for the afternoon."

Maxwell had called a pilot he knew and asked him to take us up for a few hours. As Maxwell had promised, there were no ghosts or demon hunters in sight as the small four-seater plane took off. Maxwell and I were squeezed into the cramped backseat, and we were wearing headphones so we could talk to each other and to Nick.

I had never been in such a small airplane, and I was a little nervous as we bounced around in the wind. Once I got used to the feeling, though, I relaxed and found the ride soothing. The views were spectacular. Nick flew us over downtown Savannah before heading straight for Tybee Island. From there, we turned north and flew along the coastline toward Charleston, South Carolina. I had expected to turn around and fly back to Savannah after that, but instead we landed at a small airport outside Charleston. A cab took Maxwell and me to a restaurant in the historic district (which is lovely, though in my opinion, not nearly as charming as my own Savannah). It was early for dinner, but it was exactly what I needed. For once, I didn't worry about who might be sitting next to us or what could happen in the next second.

After dinner, we returned to the Charleston airport, and Nick flew us back to Savannah. I thanked Nick half a dozen times, then thanked Maxwell half a dozen more on the drive into town. I had so needed the break from worrying.

We went to my apartment for the night, and I was surprised to see that I had four messages on my answering machine. Granted, I had been staying at Maxwell's, but I hadn't had that many messages on my home phone since The Seekers had gotten some publicity about a case we did in September.

All four messages were from the same person, and each one sounded more panicked. "I need help," the last one said. "I don't know where else to go, and I'm scared to stay in my home any longer. I'm going to stay in a hotel until this has stopped." The caller, a man named Grant Roberts, left his cell phone number and the earnest plea of, "Help me before it hurts me again."

I called Grant back immediately, simultaneously grateful for another case and concerned that it sounded like another violent haunting. Grant answered immediately. "Finally," he said after I identified myself.

"I'm sorry I couldn't call back sooner," I said. "I was on an airplane all afternoon." Why was I even apologizing to this guy? According to my answering machine, his first call had been only ninety minutes before I called him back.

"I need your team at my house as soon as possible," Grant continued. "I'm going to wind up with a broken leg or worse if this doesn't stop."

"What kind of activity have you had?" I asked.

"The painful kind. Three kitchen knives have been thrown at me, and pieces from my model car collection keep getting moved to the stairs. I've tripped so many times that I've lost count. Tell me, what am I supposed to do about that?"

Grant's tone was so accusatory that I felt like he was blaming me for the paranormal activity. I was tempted to tell him to simply avoid his kitchen and stairs. Instead, I said, "I understand you're staying at a hotel now, so you've made a wise decision. When did this activity begin?"

"Three days ago."

The same day as the increased activity at The Hex. Interesting. "Have you experienced any activity in your home prior to this?" I asked.

"Sure, but just the usual. Lights turning off and on, footsteps now and then, and the occasional slamming door. Never anything like this."

I assured Grant that I'd check with the team and try to secure a night when we could investigate. Since all of us were off work for the week, I expected that to be soon. After Grant and I spoke, I called Shaun and Carter. Both agreed that we needed to act soon, and Grant was happy when I called him back to suggest we go to his house the next night.

Normally, we like to interview clients before we investigate. It serves as a way to meet the client and decide if we really want to investigate their home or business. Some people seem fine on the phone, but their personality—or their claims—send up a red flag when we meet in person. It's nice to know those things early so we can politely decline an investigation. We don't turn people down often, thankfully. In Grant's case, we were willing to jump right in and investigate. We told ourselves that it was because he needed immediate help, but in reality I think we were all just ready for another investigation.

Daisy had to sit out this investigation, as well, so it was just me, Shaun, Carter, and Maxwell slated to arrive at Grant's house at eight o'clock on Wednesday night. Or so I had thought. Maxwell and I pulled into the driveway of Grant's house, which was in nearby Garden City, and saw Carter getting out of his car. Maxwell and I both said, "What?" when a blonde woman with long legs climbed out of the passenger side. Had Carter brought a date?

Before we went up to the front door, I hailed Carter. "Who's your friend?" I kept my voice casual, but I was inwardly shouting at him for bringing someone to my team's investigation without any notice.

"Betty Boorman, meet Kayce Williams. Kayce, Betty." Carter spoke casually, as if he brought new people along all the time. When I simply raised my eyebrows, he continued. "Kayce is a psychic. She was interested in helping us tonight."

"Oh." I decided that Kayce must be a psychic medium —able to communicate with spirits—rather than the kind who could tell the future. If she had been the latter, she would have known that I was not going to be happy about her showing up on a Seekers investigation. Still, I didn't want to be overly mean to Kayce, when I mostly blamed Carter for this situation. I at least gave Kayce a clipped hello and shook her hand, wondering how on Earth she'd managed to squeeze into her skin-tight jeans.

I strode ahead of the others as I approached the front door. I took a few deep breaths and tried to clear my mind of Carter and his new sidekick so I could concentrate on Grant Roberts and his haunting.

Grant answered the door about one second after I'd rung the doorbell. A suitcase sat in the entryway, and I guessed that he had restocked his wardrobe before returning to the hotel. "Grant, I'm Betty, it's nice to meet you," I said. Grant took my proffered hand and pulled me over the threshold. Instead of greeting me, he launched into a flurry of exclamations about how scared he was and how dangerous things were.

"Did anything happen while you were waiting for us?" I knew that Grant had only returned home to let us in.

"Yes, and it's bad. Really bad." He still sounded a little angry.

I glanced over my shoulder and saw that everyone had

followed me inside. Even Shaun had arrived. I turned back to Grant. "Are you okay? Tell us what happened."

Grant just shook his head. "No, you have to see it to believe it."

We followed as Grant led us down the hall. His split-level home looked very 1960s on the outside, but a lot of renovations had been done to the interior. Everything was sleek and modern, including the built-in shelving for Grant's model car collection, which took up an entire wall of his living room.

Grant opened the door to the master bedroom and gestured dramatically. "I found this not five minutes ago. It wasn't here when I first arrived."

I took one look at the bedroom, and then I did something I had never done before: I swore in front of a client.

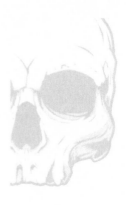

FIVE

If I had felt déjà vu at The Hex, then now I was sure I was living in some weird parallel universe. There on one wall of Grant's bedroom was my name, written over and over again in blood red paint.

Kayce gasped. "Written in blood!" Her voice was dramatic, and I was glad that my back was to her so I couldn't see the expression that, I was sure, accompanied it.

"No," Grant said, "it's just paint that I use on my cars."

I huffed out a breath. "Grant, I don't know what to say. Why the ghost would write my name all over your wall is a mystery. I'm very sorry, and I assure you I'll pay for you to repaint."

Grant shrugged. "Get this thing out of my house, and we'll call it even."

I nodded. Grant stayed with us for only a few more minutes before he left. I couldn't blame him for wanting to stay there as short a time as possible. I kind of wanted to go with him.

I felt a hand on my shoulder and looked up to see Shaun. "This is weird," I said.

Shaun just nodded. "You okay?"

"No." There was no point in lying. Just two months before, this same scene had played out at a home in the

Victorian district of Savannah. I'd been horrified then to see my name scrawled all over one wall, and I was horrified now. The first time, we had learned that the message was from the ghost Faith, and she had been trying to relay a message to me from Maxwell. Faith had been trying to help, so maybe this ghost had an important message, too. Maybe all of the recent violent activity was simply a way for the ghost to get someone's attention. Perhaps even my attention.

I relayed all of this to the others, who hesitantly agreed. Maxwell was uncomfortable with me staying in the house, and Shaun suggested that I should stick to monitoring the videos all night rather than investigating.

Carter, on the other hand, was confident that we'd have a more productive evening than we had at The Hex. "We've got Kayce with us tonight. Between her abilities and my skill, we'll get some answers."

I rolled my eyes. Carter and his damn ego. And now a psychic, too? I wasn't against the idea of using psychic mediums on investigations. I'd heard that some teams got good results with the help of psychically sensitive team members. In my experience, though, I'd never seen anything to make me think that a psychic was anything more than a good guesser who had a really strong intuition. I'd told Daisy before that if she would wander around throwing out names and methods of death, she could probably call herself a psychic, too. With her intuition, her guesses were bound to be right at least some of the time.

I gave in and volunteered to man the video monitors that we set up in the living room, at least for the first part of the evening. We generally set up our operations in the kitchen, but this time we had an infrared camera in there to see if any more kitchen knives would get thrown. We decided it would be best to keep out of there ourselves: we did not need our night ending with a trip to the Emergency Room.

Carter and Kayce volunteered to investigate the master bedroom first, though I insisted that Shaun go with them. Kayce had never been on an investigation, and I had no idea how she might react if something happened.

Maxwell took my hand and held it the entire time we sat on the couch, watching the video monitors that we had set up on the coffee table. "I should have gone up," he said. "I could probably get better answers than Carter's new friend."

"We'll let them finish up, then maybe you and Shaun can have a stab at it. Or you and Carter, if you're really brave."

Shaun, Carter, and Kayce came into the living room half an hour later, looking very disappointed. "Nothing," Shaun announced.

Maxwell stood up. "Then it's time for me to try. Carter? Shaun?"

Shaun volunteered to return to the bedroom while Carter and Kayce settled down on the couch next to me. "How did you and Carter meet?" I asked Kayce.

"At a book signing. I'm such a huge fan of his work. When Carter signed my book, I told him about my abilities, and he invited me to come on a ghost hunt some time." Kayce smiled and put her hand on Carter's thigh. "I'm really excited to be here."

I had a feeling that Kayce wanted to do more than look for ghosts tonight.

"Did you get any impressions while you were in the room?" Whether or not I believed in her "abilities," she might at least have some valuable information for us.

Kayce's lips immediately formed a thin line, and she raised her eyebrows at me. Carter, who was sitting between us, leaned back and looked slightly uncomfortable. I knew this wasn't going to be pleasant.

"I do have a theory," Kayce said. "Carter told me about that music club, and how you were the only one the ghost whispered to. He also mentioned that someone's hair was caught on fire, just like yours had at a ghost hunt. Then we get here, and your name is all over the wall, and supposedly that happened to you during a ghost hunt, too."

I nodded when Kayce paused, clearly waiting for me to confirm her list of incidents.

"I think you're the one doing all of this," she continued.

I sat up straight. "You what?"

Kayce put up one hand. "Now, wait, Betty, let me explain. I understand you're going through a really difficult time right now, and that you have a lot of stress." I shot my meanest look at Carter. Had he actually told her about our war with the demon hunters? "Your fear and anxiety create a lot of negative energy, and I think that energy is manifesting as all of this strange activity."

I opened my mouth to speak. When nothing came out, Carter said, "It makes sense, Betty. Poltergeist activity is often linked to teenagers because their hormonal and emotional changes create a lot of energy, which sometimes causes physical phenomena. You're going through a lot, and Kayce thinks the same thing is happening to you. Your subconscious is causing all of this to happen."

"I…you think it's poltergeist activity…centered around me?" It was ludicrous. I hadn't even known there was a band playing at The Hex on Christmas Eve, let alone that one of them had long hair and used candles. My subconscious certainly hadn't known it, either. I said as much to Carter and Kayce, though I doubt it came out quite as coherently. I was so flabbergasted by Kayce's suggestion that I was having a hard time speaking. "I'd never even heard of Grant before tonight, so how could I have caused poltergeist activity in his home?"

Kayce shrugged. "I don't know. That's for you and Carter to figure out."

"This is ridiculous," I snapped. I stood up and walked into the kitchen, where I laid my palms against the cool granite countertop and closed my eyes. If I had stayed in the living room, I probably would have said something I'd regret.

I could feel my arms trembling and knew that I was only getting angrier. I was angry with Carter, with Kayce, and even with myself for being in such a state that anyone would even suggest I was manifesting poltergeist activity. I agreed with Carter's theory that poltergeists weren't actually ghosts, but the result of excess energy, usually generated by a person. Energy needs to be released somehow, and sometimes it is released through physical means, such as books moving or loud noises.

A soft rattling noise began, and I thought that my shaking arms were vibrating something on the kitchen counter. I dropped my arms down by my side and opened my eyes. The rattling continued. I followed the sound and saw that two kitchen knives were quivering in their butcher's block. I had just enough time to register what was about to happen when a pair of arms grabbed me and threw me to the floor.

Maxwell was on top of me, my body pinned by his. My head was crushed against his chest, and the only way I knew it was him was by his warmth and his familiar touch. I hadn't even seen him materialize in the kitchen with me.

There was a loud clanging sound as one of the knives went flying and landed on the floor. At the same time, I heard a grunt from Maxwell, and his arms tightened around me.

"Betty, what's going on?" I heard Carter walking into the kitchen. "Maxwell!" Carter's tone wasn't one of surprise at finding Maxwell in the kitchen, but one of concern.

Maxwell finally lifted away from me, settling awkwardly into a cross-legged position on the floor. Carter approached him and reached out, as if he wanted to help, but he stopped short. "What do I need to do?" Carter asked.

Maxwell grimaced. "Pull it out."

I stood up just in time to see Carter yank one of the kitchen knives out of Maxwell's back. I uttered a horrified, "Oh!" while Kayce, who had followed Carter, screamed.

If Maxwell hadn't shown up when he did, that knife would have been in me, and I wouldn't have gotten back up like Maxwell did. That thought paralyzed me for a moment: here I was, always worrying about the demon hunters, and it was a ghost that had very nearly killed me.

I couldn't think about that right now. I forced my feet to move and grabbed a kitchen towel to press against Maxwell's back. He would heal, I knew, but all the blood seeping across the back of his shirt was still disconcerting.

Shaun had joined us by then, and I heard Carter issuing instructions to find a first-aid kit.

"You can't just put a bandage over that!" Kayce said. She sounded like she was on the verge of hysterics. "We need to call an ambulance!"

I looked up in time to see Carter raise a warning finger. "No ambulances. He'll be fine."

"But—"

"No." Carter's tone was firm. I was used to hearing him issue orders, but not like this. All trace of his usual arrogance was gone, replaced by a cold efficiency.

Carter handed me a fresh towel. Maxwell was still

bleeding profusely, but he sat calmly, breathing slowly and evenly.

"How do you feel?" I asked. It was a silly question; of course he felt terrible.

"Grateful." Well, that wasn't the answer I'd been expecting. Maxwell's voice was quiet, and I leaned forward to hear him as he continued. "I knew it was going to happen. The ghost was purposely staying away from me, I could tell, but he practically shouted, 'Throw the knives at her!' I instantly came down here."

"Just in time, too," I said. "I'm glad you overheard the ghost, or I'd be dead right now."

Maxwell nodded. "We need to leave. All of us."

I couldn't argue. Shaun and Carter packed up while I continued to tend to Maxwell. Before we left, we cleaned up the kitchen. Luckily, the towels had soaked up most of the blood. We left a clean kitchen, but I owed Grant Roberts a couple of new towels. I also owed Grant an explanation about the paranormal violence at his house, which I wouldn't be able to deliver.

Maxwell walked slowly out to my car, and instead of sitting in the front seat, he climbed into the back. He insisted on sitting sideways so he wouldn't smear blood all over the upholstery.

I drove home slowly, looking anxiously in my rearview mirror after every bump we hit. I didn't want Maxwell to get jostled too much. "I wonder what Carter is going to tell his psychic friend," Maxwell said as we neared the historic district. His voice already sounded stronger. "She must really be wondering."

"Carter shouldn't have brought her, anyway. At least, not without asking me first. He can tell her whatever he wants, as long as it's not the truth." I hesitated to tell Maxwell my suspicion that Carter had already filled Kayce in on our situation with the demon hunters. For all Carter knew, Kayce could be on their side. It wasn't safe to talk to anybody.

I parked in the alley behind my apartment and helped Maxwell ease out of the back seat. It looked like the blood had stopped spreading, which meant that his wound was already closing.

When I opened my front door, it felt strangely silent inside. Mina usually came out to greet me, and Lieutenant Griffin often banged on the window blinds to say hello. I dropped my keys on the table by the door and headed for the bathroom: I knew Maxwell would want to shower off all the blood before I got him bandaged up.

I realized that Maxwell wasn't behind me, and I turned to wait for him. He was standing just outside the front door, a dismayed expression on his face. He stared straight inside, like he could see something I couldn't.

"Maxwell?" I prompted.

"I can't come inside."

"Why not?"

Maxwell raised a hand and pressed it toward the space where the front door sat when it was closed. He snatched his hand back with a hiss. "They've been here."

He didn't even have to tell me who "they" were. I knew instinctively that he was referring to demon hunters.

"That doesn't explain why you can't come in." I was walking toward the door now, as if I might be able to pull Maxwell inside.

"It does explain it. They've consecrated your apartment. It's holy ground now, and I can't come in."

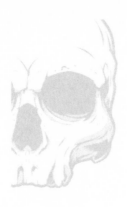

SIX

It took a moment for Maxwell's statement to sink in. If the hunters had brought a priest out to consecrate my home, then that meant they might have done the same to Maxwell's house. It also meant that the hunters knew Maxwell was spending the majority of his time at my place.

"Lieutenant Griffin!" I called. There was no answer. "Lieutenant!"

I moved to the center of my living room, turning in a circle as I continued to call Lieutenant Griffin. "You can come out now, the demon hunters are gone." Still, there was no answer.

"He's not here," Maxwell said quietly.

"What do you mean? He can't go anywhere."

Maxwell shook his head sadly at me. "His presence is gone, Betty. He was probably exorcised when they consecrated the building."

I instantly felt tears begin to form. Lieutenant Griffin had only been with me for a few months, but he had been a friend and a protector. I liked having him around, and I had a real fondness for him. He had even helped me rescue Maxwell from Tage. Plus, I realized, the lieutenant was the first present Maxwell had ever given me. Now he was gone, and I hadn't even been here to help him cross over.

I sniffed and wiped at my eyes. It was silly to grieve for a man who was already dead, I knew, but I couldn't help it. Still, Maxwell and I had to make some quick decisions. I would have time to mourn for Lieutenant Griffin later, once we were safe.

"They're probably still near here, watching," I said. "We need to get out of here now."

Before I locked up, I found Mina and scooped her up. She joined me in the front seat while Maxwell climbed in the back again. "Where to?" I asked as I pulled out of the alley.

"I would say we should go to my house, but they may have done the same there."

"Or they could be waiting for us to show up there so they can attack."

"Park about two blocks from the house. We can walk over and take a peek," Maxwell suggested.

"You're a little conspicuous right now," I reminded him. "You can wait in the car, and I'll go take a peek."

"No. It's too dangerous."

"I'll be sneaky. I promise."

Maxwell reluctantly agreed, and I pulled into a curbside parking spot two streets over from Maxwell's. I walked over, but instead of going down Maxwell's street, I turned into the alley that ran behind his townhouse. The alley gave access to Maxwell's garage, which was the old carriage house behind his home. I would be able to see if any lights were on in his house from half a block away.

Before I ever looked up at the windows, though, I saw a familiar pickup truck parked in the alley, blocking the garage door. It belonged to Lou Miles.

My heart sank. Not only had the hunters beat us here, but Lou was with them. My former friend was participating in the hunters' revenge. They had made my apartment inhospitable for Maxwell, and they expected us to

49

take refuge here. The house would be surrounded, and every hunter would be armed with consecrated weapons, ready to pierce Maxwell's heart to send him to hell. As for me, well, those weapons would work just as well on a human.

I should have turned and left right then. Maxwell was alone and injured, and he could be in danger. I could be in danger, too. Instead of being scared, though, I felt my anger flare. I stalked straight toward Lou's truck. The alley was dimly lit, but I could see his silhouette behind the wheel. When he finally spotted me walking toward him, he revved his engine and began to pull forward. He wasn't trying to hit me, I realized. He just wanted to get away. If I was alone, then that meant Maxwell was elsewhere, and there would be no demon-banishing reward money for Lou.

I stood in the middle of the alley, my fists clenched at my sides and my eyes looking straight at Lou's headlights.

Lou kept driving toward me, but I held my ground. I was too angry to feel any fear. Finally, Lou braked hard and screeched to a halt. I walked up to his driver's side window. It was open, and I reached inside to grab his arm with both hands.

"You killed him!" I shouted.

"I haven't killed anyone." Lou sounded both angry and scared, and he leaned as far away from me as he could.

I shoved my head through the window so that my face was only inches from Lou's. "Yes, you did! Lieutenant Griffin is gone because of what you did to my apartment!"

Lou frowned. "Are you talking about your ghost?"

"Yes. When you consecrated my apartment, it exorcised him. He's gone, and it's your fault!" I shook Lou's arm as I spoke.

"Betty, he was already dead. If he crossed over, then that's a good thing. He will be at peace."

"He didn't want to be at peace. He wanted to protect me."

Lou's voice was quiet when he spoke again. "You're so selfish. It's always about what you want: your ghost, your demon. You're willing to sacrifice everything that's right so you can be happy."

I gasped and backed my head out of the truck. Lou's words stung. I wanted to retort, to tell him that he'd thrown in his lot with a group that didn't care if innocent people got hurt or even killed. The hunters had even used revenants—dead bodies haunted by their own spirits—in their fight against us. How was that any better than me having Lieutenant Griffin as my Spirit Sentry?

I couldn't say any of that, though. I was too hurt by Lou's words and too aware of his restrained anger. I hated fighting with him, and I hated knowing that he'd lost the respect he once had for me. Was he right about me being selfish? If I hadn't wanted Maxwell so badly, I wouldn't have lost Lou's friendship.

Lou waited for me to respond. When I didn't, his chest heaved. I thought he was about to shout at me, but instead he sighed heavily. "I don't like it either, Betty. I miss you, and believe me when I say that I only want what's best for you."

"But you and the other hunters are here to kill me and Maxwell."

"Not you, no. I'd never let them kill you." Lou regarded me for a long moment, and then he put his truck in reverse and began to back away.

I watched Lou as the truck rolled backwards, which was why I saw his eyes widen in panic just before two hands locked around my throat.

I struggled against the man behind me, but his hands stayed tight around my neck. The edges of my vision turned black, and I knew I would pass out if I didn't get air

51

soon. Still, I continued to fight even as my limbs began to feel heavy.

Lou's truck came to a stop, and I heard his car door slam. Was he coming to help my attacker or me? One thought stood out clearly in my mind: use your feet. I stomped down hard on the man's foot twice, using all the force I could muster. He howled in pain, but his grip only loosened slightly. My timing was perfect, though: he was distracted just enough that he didn't see Lou running at him. Lou crashed into him, and all three of us tumbled to the ground.

"What are you doing?" The man was another hunter, I was sure. His hands slid from my throat as he turned his attention to Lou.

As I scrambled away on my hands and knees, I heard Lou say, "Not Betty."

I didn't wait to find out how the fight ended. I finally recovered my breath enough that I could stand and run unsteadily to the mouth of the alley. Once I regained the street, I slowed down but continued to move. I had to get back to my car before anyone could follow me.

"That was quick," Maxwell said when I opened the car door. I hadn't even been gone for ten minutes. "Is it safe?"

"No." I was surprised by how raspy my voice was. I didn't stop to explain anything to Maxwell. I just started the car and pulled into traffic.

"Betty? What happened? Are you okay?"

"Yes."

Maxwell laid his hand on my shoulder. "Are you hurt?"

"No."

Maxwell fell silent, and I drove south, not really thinking about where I was going. I just knew that we had to get away from Maxwell's house and the hunters. We were sitting at a red light when Maxwell spoke again, his voice barely above a whisper. "Lou was there."

"How did you know?" My throat ached, and talking hurt.

"Because you're not saying anything. If it had just been some hunter, you would be angry or scared right now. But this silence…only someone who was your friend could make you feel like this."

I put my head down on the steering wheel and sighed. My heart ached more than my throat. I looked up again just as the light turned green. "He helped me, though," I whispered. "It was another hunter who attacked me, and Lou tackled him."

"I shouldn't have let you go by yourself."

I shrugged. "Maybe it's for the best. They might have attacked you instead. If they start fighting with each other, they won't have as much time to fight us."

"Or as organized of an effort. Where are we going, anyway?"

I started to answer that I didn't know before I realized that I was heading for Shaun and Daisy's house. I didn't want to put them in danger, but Maxwell and I both needed somewhere to rest and think so we could decide what to do. We were both homeless for the time being.

We must have looked like a sad trio on the front steps. Shaun opened the door to find me—dirty and half-strangled with a meowing cat in my arms—and Maxwell, who looked perfectly fine from the front but resembled a walking corpse from the back.

Shaun didn't even speak. He just ushered us inside, shut the door, and locked it.

Daisy ambled into the living room, wearing hot pink pajamas and yawning widely. She was fully awake when Maxwell turned to Shaun, and she got a view of his back. "Shaun told me you got stabbed, but I didn't think it would have bled so much." Daisy instantly began fussing over Maxwell, instructing him to take off his shirt.

Maxwell put his hand on Daisy's as she reached out to begin unbuttoning his shirt for him. "You're definitely going to be a very attentive mother," he said, "but you need to hear this before you start nursing me back to health."

I slumped down on the couch while Shaun got me a glass of water. Daisy turned her attention to me finally and saw the red marks on my throat. "Oh, Boo. Are you all right? Shaun, you didn't tell me that Betty got hurt, too."

"She didn't. At least, not on the investigation." Shaun and Daisy sat down across from me, but Maxwell remained standing, too afraid of getting bloodstains on the furniture. Instead, he positioned himself next to me, one hand on my shoulder like he was afraid to let me out of his sight again.

We explained what had happened at my apartment and at Maxwell's house. Daisy was furious when I repeated Lou's accusation that I was selfish. "After all you've been through with him," she began, "and he has the audacity to call you selfish. Did he ever consider that he's the one being selfish for doing this to you? He's so eager to banish Maxwell that he's not even concerned about breaking your heart."

"Maybe he's right, Daisy. Maybe I am selfish."

"Don't talk like that. He might have saved your life tonight, but he can still play mind games with you. Don't you dare start to doubt yourself." Daisy looked as indignant as she could with pajamas and bed head.

"But here I am with nowhere to go, looking for help from you. That's terribly selfish of me, because it puts both of you in danger."

Daisy stood up and crossed her arms. "Those hunters wouldn't dare to mess with a pregnant lady. As long as I'm with you, you're safe."

It sounded ridiculous, but Daisy had a good point. Some hunters had a very narrow sense of morality, but harming a mother-to-be had to be too extreme for even the worst of the hunters.

Shaun agreed, adding, "You can stay in the guest room as long as you need to. Betty, you can borrow some of Daisy's clothes if you think it's too dangerous to go home. Maxwell, I'd offer the pick of my wardrobe to you, but I'm afraid you'd be too horrified to go out in public in my clothes."

Maxwell raised his eyes to the ceiling. "We all have to make sacrifices," he intoned.

While Maxwell showered, Daisy sat me down in the kitchen and gave me a glass of milk and a stack of graham crackers. "They'll make you feel better," she promised.

"Maxwell is right; you're going to be a really good mom."

Daisy's smile faded when she sat down next to me. "I hope so, and I hope that you and Maxwell are both there to see me in action. I'm worried about both of you, Boo."

"Me, too. I'm even worried about Carter." I took a bite of graham cracker, then sat up straight. "Carter! I forgot all about him!"

I pulled out my cell phone and was still trying to swallow my mouthful of cracker when Carter answered. "Are you okay?" I said, skipping right over saying hello.

"I think so. Why?" Carter's voice was slow and muffled. He had been sound asleep.

"I was attacked by a demon hunter tonight." I filled Carter in on everything that had happened since we left the investigation at Grant's house.

All Carter had to say when I finished was, "I'm glad that Lou isn't as bad as we thought."

"Carter, did you understand anything I just said? You are probably being watched, too, and they might attack you next."

"My security alarm is on." Carter yawned. "I'll look

out the windows and see if anyone is lurking, but I'm guessing they're more interested in you and Maxwell. Besides, if Lou and another hunter got into a fight tonight, they might be taking a break to let things cool off between them."

"Well, just be careful, okay?" Carter promised me that he'd exercise more caution before I let him go back to sleep.

Maxwell was done showering by then, and he came into the kitchen wearing nothing but a pair of Shaun's pajama pants. He had a roll of gauze in one hand and medical tape in the other. Wordlessly, he handed them to me and turned around.

The gash from the knife looked a lot better already with the blood washed away, and it looked like it was quickly healing. Still, I taped gauze in place while I told Daisy and Maxwell about Kayce's theory that I was causing poltergeist activity.

"No," Maxwell said firmly. "The Hex and Grant's house are haunted. Remember, I could feel the ghosts there with us."

"The ghosts might be there, but maybe it really is my sub-conscious manifesting all of this activity," I argued. "The ghost at The Hex might have told me to get out because my brain is causing problems at his bar. I have been under a lot of stress lately, so Kayce's theory makes some sense."

"I'm with Maxwell," Daisy said. "Poltergeist activity occurs close to the person who is giving off the excess energy. The activity happens in the home where the person lives, not halfway across town."

"Then why did that wall at Grant's have my name on it?" I didn't want to believe that all of this was my fault, but at the same time, I knew that it wasn't just coincidence.

"Maybe the ghost has a message for you. It could also

be a warning." Daisy looked thoughtful. "You were at Grant's while Lieutenant Griffin was being exorcised. Maybe the ghost was trying to tell you."

"Maybe." I didn't think that was the reason, but I was too tired to argue, and every word I spoke stung my throat.

As tired as I was, I took a shower before going to bed. I joked that I wanted to wash all of the demon hunter off of me, but that wasn't far from the truth. I wanted to put as much hot water and as many soapsuds between me and the attack as I could. As always, I took off my necklace before I stepped into the shower. A St. Michael medallion hung from the chain, a gift from Lou for protection from demons. Instead of putting it back on after my shower, though, I tucked it into the back corner of a drawer.

Maxwell was peering out the curtained window when I joined him in the guest bedroom. "I hope we can at least get through the rest of the night without an attack," I said.

"I think that's a safe assumption. I do, however, plan to pop outside once in a while to check things out. Don't worry, I'll wait until you're asleep before I do."

I slid under the covers and waited for Maxwell to join me. When he did, I rolled onto my side and put my head on his chest. "I'm almost relieved," I said. "The anticipation of an attack was so bad that I feel better now that it's finally started."

It was true, but I also felt terribly sad. I sniffed and felt the first tears begin to slide down my cheeks. Crying still hurt my throat, but I couldn't hold back any longer. I mentally kicked myself for being so weepy. Why did I have to cry so much?

Maxwell stroked my hair, but he didn't try to quiet me. He knew I needed to get it out of my system. Instead, he said, "At least he came to your aid tonight."

"You are psychic," I said. How did Maxwell know that I was thinking of Lou?

"No, I just know that his friendship meant a lot to you. I'm sorry he said those things to you."

"He'd banish you without a second thought. He once said he'd only come after you if you broke up with me or treated me badly."

"But I did break up with you."

"Well," I said, "but we're back together now. I guess it doesn't matter to Lou anymore."

Maxwell's voice was subdued when he said, "We changed the rules. You and I both killed a hunter."

"I know. I worry about him, though. This isn't Lou. He's not this vengeful person."

Maxwell tightened his arms around me. "Hopefully he'll realize that before it's too late."

I didn't know what Maxwell meant by that. Before it was too late could either mean before Lou killed Maxwell or before Maxwell killed Lou. Both options had repercussions that I didn't want to think about, so I didn't ask. As I drifted to sleep, though, I prayed that Lou would be able to forgive me, even if I was selfish.

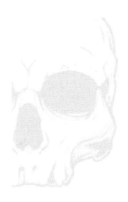

SEVEN

I didn't want to get out of bed on Thursday morning. I had slept fitfully, waking up after every nightmare. Twice, Maxwell was gone, and I waited for him to reappear before I could fall asleep again.

Maxwell's vigilance was unnecessary. As I had hoped, we got through the night without another attack.

Daisy already had a pot of coffee on when I trudged into the kitchen. I mumbled good morning and didn't speak again until I began my second cup. "Your throat looks better than I expected," Daisy offered encouragingly. "I had thought the bruising would be worse."

"I can't remember a time when I was uninjured," I said. "I'm still healing from all of my Serenity Island battle scars."

"Oh, you know the saying, 'Demons dig scars.'" Daisy smiled and shoved a plate of pancakes in front of me. "Speaking of demons, how is yours?"

"Still sleeping. He kept going outside last night to keep an eye on things. I don't think he got much rest. At least his back should be fine by now."

"Well, I don't know what you have planned for today, but whatever you're doing is what I'm doing. I'm taking this pregnant lady defense seriously. And Shaun says he's not leaving me unprotected, and I know Maxwell won't be leaving you alone, so it looks like we're all in it together."

"Great, I have an entourage now." I smiled wanly. "We should go over the evidence from last night, and I need to get food and litter for Mina."

By the time Maxwell finally got up, we were already halfway through the EVP sessions from Grant's house. Shaun and Maxwell's session hadn't yielded anything, which we had expected since Maxwell had sensed that the ghost wanted to be as far from him as possible.

I didn't anticipate finding anything from Carter and Kayce's EVP session, either. Shaun had been in the room with them, but he had remained silent, allowing Kayce to ask a string of questions. They ranged from perfectly acceptable to the downright weird, like "What's your favorite color?" and "What's your sign?"

I could only shake my head and laugh. Carter had certainly found himself a ridiculous woman.

But it was Kayce's final question that really surprised me. "Why don't you like Betty?" she asked. What kind of a question was that? Sure, the ghost had scrawled my name all over the wall, but that didn't mean I was disliked.

A child's voice answered the question, breathy but full of ire. "Bad, bad, bad," it said.

The others were listening to the young boy's voice, too, but I was the only one who got chills. Did the ghost think I was bad? Or was Kayce bad for even asking the question? Or, I considered, maybe the child was referring to himself.

Maxwell thought a fourth possibility was the most likely. "The boy is referring to some outside influence that made him this way. He throws knives, tries to trip Grant, and doesn't like anyone coming into his home. He's angry or agitated for some reason."

"But what could that reason be?" Daisy asked. "Why did he suddenly become violent?"

"We could ask the same about the ghost at The Hex," Shaun added.

"Lieutenant Griffin once told me that ghosts can sometimes communicate with each other," I said. "Maybe there's a ghost that's causing trouble, some kind of spiritual disruption."

"If that's the case, then I certainly hope he doesn't get any other spirits upset," Daisy said. "The injury list is long enough already." My phone rang just as Daisy said the last word. "I spoke too soon," she added.

"You don't know that this is about another violent haunting," I said.

Daisy just pursed her lips and gave me her most effective "we'll see who's right" look.

The caller was a man named Giancarlo Maletta, and his smooth voice had just a hint of an accent. "I understand that you are a ghost hunter," he said.

"I am. Were you referred to us?"

"Yes. You were at The Hex recently, although I understand you didn't have much luck there. I hope you will have more success at my house."

"What have you been experiencing?"

"I have been seeing things. People in my bedroom, in the basement. I see them for just a split second, and then they are gone. I would like to know why it is happening and who they are. And, if possible, maybe you can help them move on."

I smiled into the phone. This sounded perfect: a nice, normal haunting. No violence. No crazy messages. Just an apparition or two.

I assured Giancarlo that we could be at his house the next night. "My team is here with me, and they're all nodding their heads that tomorrow works," I said.

When I got off the phone, I described the haunting. "See, Daisy, it's not another violent haunting."

"We don't know that. He may not be telling you the whole story. We're supposed to go meet with potential clients first, remember?" Daisy was giving me another stern look.

"I know, but after weeks of no investigations, this is such a nice change of pace." When Daisy continued to stare me down, I added, "Okay, maybe I'm getting a little too eager."

———

I really was a little too eager, but I mostly blamed that on the fact that I was practically a prisoner in the house. Despite what Daisy had said about all of us sticking together, Shaun left to run errands, promising to pick up cat food and litter for Mina, as well as toothbrushes and other toiletries for Maxwell and me. Maxwell bravely tried materializing to his house so he could at least wear his own clothes. His attempts failed, confirming his fear that his home had been consecrated. Maxwell would have to bear with wearing Shaun's clothes, a fate he lamented more than the loss of his house. At least his garage hadn't been consecrated, so he was able to get his Audi R8 back.

Before I could call Carter about joining us for the investigation, he called me. "Something's not right," he said when I answered.

My eyes turned to the front door, as if I would find hunters on the doorstep. "Tell me," I said.

"I'm being watched. I could tell something wasn't right when I left my place this morning. Someone was standing on the corner of my block, watching me. I walked over to the coffee shop to meet my dad, and the guy followed me the whole way there and the whole way back."

"Is he still outside your house?" I had never been to Carter's house, but I knew it was a nicely restored historic home not too far from my apartment. It had been a gift from his dad when Carter graduated from college.

"I don't know. I can't see the corner without walking out the front door. I'm not sure whether I should just sit tight or try to slip away."

"I don't know, either," I said, "but Daisy suggested last night that they might be trying to play mind games. They're trying to make us nervous and doubtful. My vote is that you do whatever will give you the most peace of mind."

"Right. Good idea."

"What are you going to do, then?"

"I have no idea."

I laughed as a sudden thought struck me. "It's too bad you're not still being filmed for that reality show. No one would dare attack you with cameras rolling."

Carter was silent for a moment. "That's brilliant," he finally said.

"You're kidding, right? I didn't mean it."

"No, it's perfect. I'll call Mick and Dwayne and see if they can come right away. We were going to wait until the end of January to start up again, but—"

"You mean you were going to keep filming?" I was appalled. After the events on Serenity Island, Carter had called the two cameramen who had been there working with us. Carter had given them some excuse about the preservation team hitting a snag and rescinding their permission to feature the old island resort. After such a disastrous start, I couldn't believe that Carter was still planning to move forward with the show.

Actually, I could believe it. And the more I thought about it, the more I realized that the idea did have merit. Mick and Dwayne were in no danger from the hunters. In fact, before everything had gone to hell on Serenity Island, the hunters had made sure that Mick and Dwayne were safely away. They had lost their equipment in the ordeal, but they hadn't lost their lives.

"Fine, Carter," I said. "Just be there tomorrow night, with or without cameras."

"Be where tomorrow night?"

I had been so sidetracked by Carter's plan that I had forgotten to tell him about the investigation. I filled him in, made him promise not to bring Kayce, and hung up.

"Be forewarned," I said, turning to the others. "Carter has a plan, and he will expect all of us to look our prettiest for it."

The only one who didn't like Carter's plan was Maxwell, who was hesitant about showing up on television. "It's a reality show starring Carter," I argued, "so I doubt anyone will watch it. No one will ever see you."

"You know better," Daisy said. "Carter has a lot of fans, and no one is better at publicity than him. I'm surprised he didn't send out a press release about his battle with the demon hunters on Serenity Island."

Daisy was right, and in the end, Maxwell decided it might be better for him to position himself somewhere outside Giancarlo's home so he could ensure that we didn't have any unwanted visitors during the evening. He wouldn't wind up on TV, and we would have an extra barrier of protection.

The rest of the day was agonizingly boring. I couldn't go anywhere, and I had nothing to do. I did, at least, get a call from Annie at The Hex. She reported that the violent paranormal activity had slowed some, but it hadn't died down altogether. A singer had walked into the green room to find his guitar smashed on the floor just the night before.

Annie hadn't been happy with me when I'd called her

after our investigation there. Shaun had emailed her the video footage of the strange attack in the green room, but we had been unable to offer any explanations. As it turned out, she was calling me again to offer a compromise.

"If you and your team don't have any plans for New Year's, why don't you come to The Hex?" she suggested. "I'll add you to the guest list so you don't have to pay the cover. It should be safer for you to be there when the place is packed, but you might still be able to find some answers."

I wasn't sure it would be safer, but I hesitantly agreed. After all, we could just leave if any strange activity occurred. We wouldn't have to pack up any equipment, either.

By the time we left for Giancarlo's house on Friday evening, I was positively stir crazy. I'd been stuck inside Daisy and Shaun's house for two days. Despite Maxwell's assurances that the hunters weren't watching the house, no one would let me even step foot on the front porch.

I borrowed Daisy's spare Savannah Spirit Seekers tee-shirt, but squeezing into a pair of her jeans was impossible. She was a petite woman, while I had a few more curves. Instead, I washed the jeans I'd arrived in and wore them again. All traces of my tumble in the alley behind Maxwell's were gone after a little elbow grease and stain remover.

The four of us drove to Giancarlo's house together, and there was a collective "wow" when we pulled into the driveway. Giancarlo lived in a neighborhood off of Victory Drive. It was south of the historic district, and it was still full of beautiful old homes. Giancarlo's had to be one of the biggest. It was practically a plantation home, with two stories and wide white columns across the front porch. Maxwell dematerialized from the passenger seat, promising that he would be out of sight but close by the entire night.

I had thought the house was impressive, but it was nothing compared to Giancarlo himself. He answered the door wearing a black tailored suit that rivaled anything Maxwell or Carter wore. His dark hair swept back from his tall forehead, and his skin was smooth and flawless.

"Hello," he said easily. "You must be Betty."

"Giancarlo," I said, extending my hand.

"Just call me Carlo." His touch was soft, but his grip was firm. And warm. Really warm.

My breath caught in my throat. Was Carlo a demon? He certainly felt like it. Even as he waved us into the house, introducing himself to Daisy and Shaun as they crossed the threshold, I was staring keenly at Carlo, trying to tell just by looking at him if he was a demon.

No, I told myself, surely he's not. Why would a demon need our help dealing with a haunting? They were capable of doing that themselves. Maybe Carlo had been holding a cup of hot coffee before he'd answered the door. I didn't see a coffee cup anywhere, but I held onto that theory, anyway.

The interior of the house was as nice as the façade, and we were ushered into a living room that had been tastefully decorated with antiques. I sat down on the couch and was surprised when Carlo sat next to me. "I assume you would like to hear more about my ghosts," he began. He addressed everyone, but his eyes were focused on me.

Daisy had already pulled out a notebook and pen. As our case manager, she was usually the one who conducted interviews with potential clients. Since we hadn't done an advance interview with Carlo, she was determined to do so now. If anything sent up a red flag in Daisy's mind, I knew she wouldn't hesitate to walk right out of there, taking Shaun and me along with her.

"Tell us, Carlo," Daisy said politely, "when did the activity begin?"

"Oh, my home has always been haunted. The previous owners even warned me that I would occasionally walk through a cold spot or have problems with electrical appliances." Carlo settled back against the couch cushions, and I turned my body so that I could face him fully. He was very handsome, and he moved and spoke with the air of someone who had grown up with a lot of money and influence.

Carlo opened his mouth to continue, but the doorbell interrupted us. It was Carter, and when he entered the living room, he smiled and winked at me.

"Please, continue," Daisy prompted as Carlo returned to his seat.

"Yes, as I was saying, activity in this house is nothing new. But a few days ago, I began to actually see the ghosts. I woke up in the middle of the night and saw a girl standing at the foot of my bed. The next day, I went into the basement and saw a man in the shadows. I have seen the girl in my bedroom every night for the past three nights."

"What does the girl look like?" Daisy was scribbling away in her notebook.

"Young. A teenager, maybe. Her hair is long and brown, and she's wearing a white dress, or a nightgown. She doesn't move; she just stares at me for a few seconds and disappears."

"And the man in the basement?"

"I could hardly tell. Big, broad. I only saw him for a split second, and then he was gone."

"Can you show us the bedroom and basement?" Shaun said. He looked anxious to start.

Daisy shook her head slightly and laid a hand on Shaun's arm. "What else has been happening?" Daisy addressed Carlo, and now her voice had an edge to it.

"That is all. Seeing two ghosts is quite enough to warrant an investigation, I should think."

"Of course it is," I interjected. Daisy was usually really polite to clients, but her voice and expression implied that she didn't believe Carlo. I didn't want him to be offended.

Daisy smiled then, glancing reassuringly at me before returning her attention to Carlo. "You'll have to excuse me, Carlo. We've met with some unusually violent ghosts lately, and I had suspected that this haunting might be similar. I just wanted to make sure it really was safe for us here."

"You may be assured of it."

And then I realized why Daisy had been so insistent. If this investigation was going to be anything like the past two, then she didn't need to be with us. She wasn't ensuring our safety, but the safety of her baby.

"I expect you would like to see where the ghosts have appeared?" Carlo stood up gracefully, but as I rose next to him, Carter cleared his throat.

"Actually, if you can wait a moment," he said, "there's something I'd like to address."

If Carter had Kayce hiding out in the hallway, then I was going to strangle him. The hunter at Maxwell's had given me a pretty good lesson in how to do it properly.

Instead, Carter brought up the subject of his reality show. After explaining it to Carlo, Carter said, "My film crew is outside. There are just two of them, if you're willing to let them film the investigation."

Carlo smiled graciously. "Of course. They are welcome to film."

Two minutes later, Carter ushered Mick and Dwayne into the house. They put down their equipment, and before I could even say hello, Mick thrust a clipboard into Daisy's hands. "You'll all have to sign one of these forms, please."

Daisy and Shaun signed the release forms that said they gave their permission to appear on TV while I shook hands with Mick and Dwayne. "I didn't expect to see you two again," I said. "I'm glad you could make it."

"Betty, it's really good to see you," Dwayne said. "Carter had said you would be here. We never got to properly say good-bye."

"Yeah, that whole adventure ended…abruptly," I said carefully. I wasn't sure what Carter had told them about our own departure from Serenity Island, but whatever it was, I knew it wasn't the truth.

"We've been in stranger situations, believe me," Mick said. I was tempted to ask what could be stranger than a remote island full of revenants, but I wasn't sure I wanted to know.

Everyone, even Carlo, was handed a small microphone to clip to their shirts. I was used to feeding the wire and battery pack down the back of my shirt and clipping it in place on the waist of my jeans. I gave Daisy and Shaun a hand once I'd gotten my own mic in place.

Before I turned my mic on, I leaned toward Carter and whispered, "How did they get here so fast?"

"I flew them first-class and promised to pay for all of the equipment they had to replace." Mick and Dwayne had left everything behind on Serenity Island, and I knew that Carter must have written a very big check. He definitely wanted his peace of mind, though I doubted that Mick and Dwayne knew they were an odd sort of security detail for Carter.

Finally, Carlo led us to the basement. Actually, Mick led the way, backing down the basement steps so he could film all of us walking into the room. If the basement had any spookiness to it, I was far too distracted to notice. I was busy worrying that Mick would trip and fall down the stairs.

The basement was finished and set up as a storage area for old furniture and a tall stack of storage bins. It was well-lit and felt perfectly ordinary. "I saw the man over there," Carlo said, pointing to a space between a matching dresser and vanity. "When I turned on the light at the top of the stairs, I saw him for just a moment."

Shaun quickly identified a good place for one of our infrared cameras to go, and then we headed up to the second floor to see Carlo's lavish bedroom. It looked like something from a movie set. The antique furniture was ornately carved, and a rich burgundy rug partially covered the dark hardwood floor. The walls were painted the same color as the rug, and several old oil paintings were hung in gilt frames. I had stepped out of a plantation house and into a castle.

"This is my bedroom," Carlo said, his eyes on me as he spoke. It was like he was bragging or possibly flirting. I suddenly wished that Maxwell was inside with us instead of keeping guard outside.

"And you see the apparition at the foot of your bed?" I prompted.

"Yes." Carlo eased himself into a seated position on the bed, stretching his long legs out in front of him. "I wake up and she is there, standing at the footboard."

"Do you know if anyone has died in this house?" Daisy had her notebook out again.

Carlo leaned back against his pillows. "I do not know for sure, but this house is over one-hundred years old. Surely someone has died here."

If I hadn't been on house arrest, I could have gone to the Historical Society to find out. It was too bad that I hadn't been able to search through documents about the house or even old newspaper articles that might pertain to it or its residents.

Our tour over, Carlo led us downstairs to the living

room again. Dwayne asked for an interview with Carlo, so while the two of them spoke, the rest of us began to set up our equipment. Shaun and Carter placed infrared cameras in the basement and the master bedroom while Daisy and I got the table and our monitor set up in the kitchen.

"This guy has a great house. He's really handsome, too," Daisy said casually. "If you were still single, I'd be throwing you in his path as much as possible."

I lowered my voice and crouched down next to Daisy, who was seated in front of the monitor. "He felt hot when we shook hands. Did you notice?"

"No. You think he's a demon?"

"Surely he's not. Right?"

"I don't think demons need ghost hunters. Besides, he seems like a perfectly nice guy."

"So does Maxwell," I reminded Daisy.

Daisy narrowed her eyes. "Good point. I'll keep an eye on him, but I'm sure he's just as human as the rest of us."

We changed the subject when Shaun radioed from the master bedroom, asking if the camera was showing the foot of the bed. It was good timing: Carlo walked into the kitchen just a moment later.

"There is coffee in the cabinet above the dishwasher. Help yourselves," Carlo said. "I'll be at a friend's house all night, and I tend to stay up late, so please, do not hesitate to call should you need me." Carlo's eyes locked onto mine again. I guess it was normal since I was his point of contact for The Seekers, but I still felt like there was more to his look. Whether it was flirtatious or sinister—or perhaps a combination of both—I couldn't tell. Regardless, I felt a strange relief when Carlo finally left. I was ready to get the investigation underway.

Apparently, so was everyone else. I shut and locked the front door after seeing Carlo out, and by the time I returned to the kitchen, Carter was already collecting his camera and tape recorder. "You and me in the bedroom, Boo," he said.

I gave him a mock salute. "Yes, sir."

"Carter suggested that you two start since Mick and Dwayne are used to filming your investigations. He thought it would be more comfortable for them," Shaun said.

"Works for me." I grabbed my own gear and followed Carter upstairs. Mick went with us, walking backwards up the stairs to film our ascent.

"You really make me nervous, you know," I told him.

"Betty, you're supposed to pretend I'm not here," Mick scolded.

"I know, but I'll have to acknowledge your presence when you fall and break your leg."

"Don't worry about me. Just worry about you."

"Hopefully I don't have anything to worry about," I mumbled.

Carter and I sat next to each other on Carlo's bed. "I don't know that Carlo would like this," Carter said, grinning. "He seemed to like you an awful lot."

"If Carlo has a problem with you and me being on his bed together, he can take it up with Maxwell."

Mick brought the camera close to my face. "Maxwell? Is he back in the picture? You mentioned him on the island."

I looked pointedly at Carter. "I thought I heard a voice, but I'm pretending it's not there."

"And on that note, let's get started." Carter snapped off the bedside light, and we both sat quietly for a moment, allowing our eyes to adjust to the darkness. Mick stood somewhere to the left of the bed, ready to face a ghost with the same casual acceptance that he'd had with the revenants.

There was a beeping sound, and Carter leaned forward

to place his tape recorder near the foot of the bed. We introduced ourselves, and Carter began asking questions. I let my eyes roam around the room, trying to make out the shapes of the furniture.

When my gaze passed the foot of the bed, I thought I saw a brief flicker. It wasn't light, but rather dark, like a shadow. It was about five feet tall, but I couldn't make out any detail.

"Carter, was there a shadow at the foot of the bed just now?"

"I didn't see anything." Carter raised his voice and directed it toward the space in front of us. "If you're there, it's okay. We won't hurt you."

I saw another brief flicker of darkness and grabbed Carter's arm. "There," I breathed.

We both sat perfectly still and silent, but I didn't see any more shadows.

"We just want to talk to you," I said. "Please come communicate with us."

This time I saw more than a shadow. The image of a girl formed briefly at the foot of the bed, gone so quickly that I wasn't even sure I had seen her until I felt Carter sit up straight next to me. "Did you...?"

"Yes." I heard Mick walk closer to the spot where we'd just seen the apparition and fought the urge to tell him to stop. There had been something wrong with the girl's face. I wasn't sure what it was, only that it wasn't normal. Demons, I knew, could sometimes look like a ghost, but there was usually some telltale sign that gave them away. Their bodies would be deformed or their faces altered. Was Carlo dealing with a demon?

No, that didn't make sense. Carlo hadn't been attacked and hadn't felt uncomfortable, even while watching the girl stand at the foot of his bed. No demon was that passive.

Carter and I sat in silence again, and again, nothing

happened. When he started to speak, we saw the same brief image. "She's responding to our voices," I said.

"What's your name?" Carter asked. "How old are you?"

I leaned forward on the bed, peering intently into the darkness. How could we convince the girl to show herself to us for more than a moment? "We want to help you," I said.

It wasn't until the girl appeared again that I realized how close to the end of the bed I had moved. I was sitting on my knees, and her face appeared just a few feet from mine. Her mouth was open, as if she were screaming or laughing, and I finally saw what was abnormal about her face. One eye was missing completely, and the skin on the right side of her face was gray-green. Bits of skin were flaking off, like someone peeling after a sunburn.

I sat back at the same moment that Mick said, "Damn."

"Betty, that wasn't the face of a ghost." Carter's voice was tight.

"No. That was the face of a revenant." I looked toward Carter, even though I could only see his outline in the darkness. "Carlo never mentioned that his ghost was anything but a teenage girl."

"Yeah, he left out 'rotting.'"

"Ghosts don't look like corpses, though. They look like they did when they were living. At least, in my experience, they do."

"This is a new one for me, too." When I turned my gaze to the foot of the bed again, Carter and I yelped at the same time.

The girl was standing there again, only this time she lingered. Her image shimmered and came into focus the longer we watched. Her lank brown hair hung over her shoulders, and her white nightgown was bloodstained and torn. One bare arm had the same rotting color as the side of her face.

It was the ghost's expression that scared me the most. Her brow was furrowed, and she glared at us with something akin to hatred. I instinctively moved closer to Carter, as if her stare could hurt me. Her mouth began to move, contorting in exaggerated motions, like she was shouting in slow motion. I couldn't make out the words, but I knew they were accusatory and unkind. I also knew that they were directed at Carter and me.

I took a deep breath. "What do you want from us?" My voice cracked, and my question sounded more like a plea. "Why are you so angry?"

The ghost simply raised one arm, her finger pointing at me. Her mouth moved again, and I could only hope that her words would be captured on the tape recorder so we could hear them later. Otherwise, I would have no way of knowing why she was so angry with us.

The girl's arm swiveled until it pointed at Carter, and she curled her fingers until she was making a clawing motion. "She's threatening you," I said quietly.

"No kidding." Carter's sarcasm was cut short as he gasped. He coughed, and when I reached toward him, his hand found mine and clamped down tight. "Can't breathe," he said between coughs.

"What are you doing to him?" The ghost didn't answer; she just continued to stare at Carter. "Stop it! Please!"

Carter was bent over now, his back heaving as he continued to cough.

I picked up my radio and shouted into it. "Get up here now."

There was a quiet pop, and the ghost's face turned to one of surprise. She gave me one last angry look and disappeared.

The bedside lamp clicked on, and Maxwell stood there, his arms already reaching out for Carter. Maxwell thumped Carter hard on the back, and with one great heave, water gushed out of Carter's mouth.

Carter drew in a shaky breath, and his hand shook in mine. Maxwell sat down on the edge of the bed, and our eyes met while Carter still leaned forward, breathing in big gasps of air. "So much for this not being a dangerous investigation," he said.

I had been so caught up in Carter's distress that I had forgotten all about Mick. Suddenly his voice cut through the room, tinged with panic. "What the hell just happened, and where the hell did you come from?"

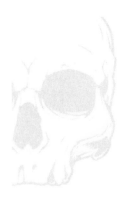

EIGHT

"Where did you come from, anyway?" I asked Maxwell. We had taken Carter downstairs, where he sank into a kitchen chair and put his head down on the table. All he would say was that he had suddenly felt as if he was drowning.

"I threw up all over the guy's bed," Carter said, interrupting Maxwell's response. I'd never heard him sound so downtrodden before.

I rubbed Carter's back slowly. He had done the same for me once, when I'd thrown up after seeing a revenant burst open. Returning the favor was the least I could do. "It was a good thing you obviously only drank water tonight instead of having dinner." It wasn't much of a comfort, I knew.

Carter just groaned in answer.

I turned my attention back to Maxwell, my eyebrows raised. We still hadn't explained his sudden appearance to Mick, who was having a hard time believing that Maxwell had just walked through the door.

"Daisy called me," Maxwell said. "She said that she felt uncomfortable, and she wanted me here in the house. I was downstairs when you radioed."

"You just came out of nowhere, man," Mick said.

"I swear he disappeared from down here," Dwayne

added, looking at Maxwell suspiciously. "No one moves that fast."

"There was a lot going on at once. I'm sure you just didn't see him run upstairs," Shaun said.

Daisy nodded. "That's right. And speaking of running, I think it's safest if I leave. I shouldn't be here."

"Of course not. You and Shaun should both go," I said. "Dwayne and Maxwell can keep an eye on the monitor here in the kitchen, and Carter and I will take Mick to the basement."

"You're actually going to tempt the other ghost?" Daisy's eyes were wide.

"We need to find out what's going on. Why did that girl appear different to us? She looked like a revenant."

"She may not have appeared differently," Carter said without raising his head from the table. "Maybe Carlo just didn't mention her appearance."

I was on the phone with Carlo the moment Daisy and Shaun left. He was as surprised as we had been about the ghost girl's state of decomposition.

"There is something more you are not telling me," Carlo said.

I hesitated. I would have to tell Carlo about the attack on Carter, but I had hoped to save it until we had some answers to go along with it. When Carlo prompted me again, I carefully told him what had happened.

Carlo's voice was grim when he spoke again. "I'm coming back to the house. I want to see what's going on."

Great. I would have a houseful of people, and not one single member of The Seekers among them. "Carlo says he's coming over," I announced.

"Then that's my cue to leave," Maxwell said. "I don't want him to show up and find a stranger here."

Maxwell used the front door, promising he'd be nearby, but not before Mick cornered him for an interview.

"So that's the infamous Maxwell," Mick said smugly, "and he is back in the picture."

"And so much for him not being on TV," was my only response.

I didn't know how long it would take Carlo to arrive, and I didn't want to wait. Carter and I went to the basement, but this time I made Mick walk all the way down the stairs before turning around to film our descent.

Since the basement was a lot cleaner and less cluttered than many I had been in, Carter and I settled comfortably onto the floor in the middle of the room. We faced the stairs, with Mick standing over us. "No one throw up this time," he said with a nervous laugh.

I pulled out my tape recorder and placed it on the floor in front of us. "My name is Betty," I began.

A stair creaked loudly.

"And my name is Carter."

The next stair down creaked.

"Please, come communicate with us," I said. "What is your name?"

Creak.

"Why are you here?"

Creak.

"Is there something you'd like to tell us?"

There was utter silence.

"How did you die?" Carter asked.

There was no response, but the hair on my arms suddenly rose, and my skin broke out in goosebumps. It felt like someone was standing right in front of me, but I couldn't see anyone in the dark.

Tentatively, I reached forward. "Can you touch me?"

I felt a wave of cold air brush against my fingers, and then a biting pain as a hand grabbed mine. Sharp fingernails dug into my skin, and I cried out. I tried to snatch my hand back, but whoever was gripping it was too strong.

I yelled again and heard Mick swearing behind me. He sounded far away. The hand began to tug, pulling my arm forward. I knew it had to be the ghost Carlo had seen here, the man he had glimpsed at the bottom of the stairs. Still, I had never known that a ghost could feel so real or be so strong.

Carter's flashlight came on. In the blinding flare of light, I saw a bald head, the scalp half torn away to reveal the skull underneath. A man's eyes stared right into mine, his intent to hurt me written clearly in his gaze. His mouth was oozing something dark, and his upper lip curled over rotten teeth.

I only saw him for an instant before he released his grip on me and disappeared. Carter shone his flashlight into every corner of the basement, but we were alone again.

"Damn, that was awful," Mick said. His voice was shaking, and I realized that it was the first time I'd ever heard him sound scared.

"You okay?" I asked.

"I should be asking you that. I could see him the whole time." With his infrared camera, Mick was able to see in the darkness, unlike Carter and me. No wonder he sounded shaken.

I looked down at my hand, which was covered in scratch marks from the ghost's nails. I shivered. "He felt so," I tried to think of the right word, "corporeal. Like an actual man grabbing me."

"We are done with this investigation," Carter said firmly. "I'm never one for running away with my tail between my legs, but you and I have both been attacked. It is time to go."

"I didn't think that filming ghosts could be more exciting than filming zombies," Mick mumbled as we trudged up the stairs.

I was surprised to run into Dwayne and Carlo in the hallway. "Why aren't you manning the monitors?" I asked.

"Carlo wanted me to show him the bedroom," Dwayne said. "It didn't look like anything was happening, so I figured you wouldn't care."

"It's his bedroom. He knows how to find it on his own," I said tersely.

Carlo smiled. "After your report, I was hesitant to go up there alone. I'm sure you understand."

Right. I hadn't thought of it that way. "I'm sorry," I said. "I'm just a little tense. You two missed a serious show just now." I put my hand out and saw that several of the scratches were slowly seeping blood. Great. First Carter threw up on Carlo's bed, and now I was going to bleed on his carpet.

"We need to get that taken care of," Carlo said. "Come with me."

I followed Carlo upstairs into his master bathroom, Carter close behind. At first I thought he wanted to keep watch over me, but instead he grabbed our infrared camera from the bedroom. "We'll be packed and ready to go by the time you get back downstairs," he promised.

Carlo's bathroom had a massive tub. I could have happily spent an hour or two soaking in it. I was so busy daydreaming of bubbles and hot water that I didn't notice Carlo approach me with an alcohol-soaked cotton ball. I flinched as the alcohol stung my scratches. "I should have warned you," Carlo said. He took my hand and swabbed again, but this time I was too distracted to feel the sting. Carlo's hand was as hot as it had been when we'd met, only this time I knew he hadn't been drinking a cup of coffee.

I looked up and was surprised to find Carlo's brown eyes looking right at me, rather than at my hand. "You're very pretty," he said. "I wouldn't think a girl like you would prefer to spend her time with ghosts."

"Why did you invite us here?" I asked abruptly.

"To investigate this haunting, of course." Carlo stopped cleaning my scratches, but his hand remained firmly over mine. My wrist and lower arm began to tingle from the heat slowly pulsing up from Carlo's hand.

"You don't need our help."

"Clearly I do. You've uncovered a very violent side to my spectral residents."

"Demons don't need help dealing with ghosts." I shifted to move away from Carlo, but he deftly stepped in front of me. I was pinned between him and the counter-top. He tilted his head downward and locked his eyes on mine. I leaned back as far as I could over the counter, but Carlo simply moved with me. I silently cursed my big mouth. I shouldn't have let Carlo know that I'd discovered his secret.

"You think I am a demon?" Carlo's voice was still smooth and controlled, and that only scared me more.

"I shouldn't have said that." I felt out of breath, and there was a surge of heat along the length of my arm.

"No, you shouldn't have. Out of curiosity, though, how did you know?"

"Your hand. It's hot."

Carlo chuckled. "You're very perceptive. Most people would never guess that my temperature gives me away. How did you learn that?"

I debated whether or not to be honest. If I told Carlo that I was dating a demon, then maybe he'd forgive me and let me go. On the other hand, it might only give him new ideas about what to do with me. What was he going to do with me, anyway? Instead of answering Carlo, I asked him just that.

"What do you plan to do with this information?" Carlo countered.

Great. We weren't going to get anywhere if we both kept asking each other questions. "You have nothing to worry about from me. The demon hunters and I don't exactly get along. I'm certainly not going to go running to them."

Carlo relaxed his grip on my hand, but he still loomed over me. My back was beginning to ache from arching backwards. I straightened up while Carlo held his ground, so our faces were only inches apart. "Why don't you get along with them?" he asked. "Aren't they here to protect pretty mortals like you?"

Now it was my turn to laugh. "One of them tried to rape me, and another one took me hostage and shot me. I'd tell you to ask them yourself, but they're both dead now."

"You killed them." It wasn't a question.

I lowered my eyes. "One of them. I'm not proud of it." I sounded like a sullen child being scolded.

"You should be. Too few of them have any real interest in saving mortals, anyway. They're too blinded by the idea of money and prestige among their peers."

"I know. And they don't care who they hurt or kill just to banish one demon."

"You have no idea how right you are." Carlo paused and finally stepped away from me. "Go home, Betty. My ghosts are only going to hurt you. I'll deal with them myself."

I wasn't going to be dismissed that easily. I was scared, but I was also curious. "Then why did you call us to come investigate in the first place?"

"I had my reasons, and I am not going to explain further. You and Carter have both been attacked tonight. Instead of asking more questions, you need to go home."

Carlo's voice was firm, and I knew he wouldn't let me learn any more of his secrets. He gestured to the door, and I dutifully made my way downstairs. As promised, Carter, Mick, and Dwayne had packed up all of the equipment already. Carlo smiled and made polite good-byes to everyone, glancing at me now and then in a silent command not to reveal his demon nature.

Mick and Dwayne had their own rental car, so we bade them goodnight. Carter was going to take Maxwell and me home. Before I could even call to let him know we were leaving, Maxwell materialized in the back seat. As Carter pulled out of the driveway, I twisted around in my seat and said, "We have a lot to talk about."

Maxwell and Carter were both concerned that the violent haunting was tied to a demon. Carlo's arrival had been perfectly timed for him to lure Dwayne away from the monitor. Had it been a coincidence, or had he been hoping to leave us stranded in the basement with an angry ghost?

"This is strange," Maxwell said. "I've never heard of demons using ghosts to do their work."

"But if you look at it from a demon's standpoint, he's doing a great job," I argued. "Fear, chaos, danger, self-doubt...I'd say he covered all the bases this evening."

"Self-doubt? What's wrong, Betty, are you afraid you're just imagining these ghosts?" Carter had certainly recovered from his earlier distress and was back to sounding as haughty as ever.

"I guess I really can't blame Carlo for that. It was Kayce who planted that seed. I wish she had never suggested that this was all a product of my subconscious." I frowned. The past three investigations had all been dangerous, and one of them had involved a demon. They had to be related to each other somehow, but I didn't know what could possibly connect them. Was it really some rogue ghost angering other paranormal entities? And if so, why did each investigation have an eerie similarity to one of my past investigations? At The Hex, someone's hair caught on fire, just as mine had at Sam MacIntosh's house. Grant Roberts had found my name written all over his bedroom wall, just like at Carla and Scott Jensen's home. And now, tonight, I was seeing ghosts that looked like revenants.

"What ties these together?" I mused.

At a confused glance from Carter, I laid out my questions. He and Maxwell didn't have an answer for me, though Maxwell wanted to materialize back to Carlo's house to confront him. Thankfully, I was able to talk Maxwell out of it. Demons aren't known for their loyalty to each other, and I didn't want Maxwell to make a new enemy. We had enough already.

Carter dropped us off at Shaun and Daisy's house, and I made him promise to call me once he was safely at home. He assured me that he would be fine since Mick and Dwayne were staying with him, but I insisted, anyway. Demons, demon hunters, and ghosts all appeared to have some sort of vendetta against us, and I was feeling more paranoid than ever.

Daisy was incensed when we told her and Shaun about Carlo's true nature and how he had anticipated the ghosts' attack on us. She wanted to go confront Carlo just as badly as Maxwell had. In this case, though, I was more concerned for Carlo's safety.

Daisy poured sweet teas for all of us, even though it was midnight and we didn't need the sugar just before bed. She realized that whatever the clock said, none of us would be sleeping anytime soon. I was too shaken, and Maxwell and Daisy were both too angry at Carlo.

Shaun was the only one who kept a calm exterior, but he didn't give the rest of us any relief when he said, "Do demons get vengeful? This started with a haunting that mimicked what that demon did at Sam's house. You concentrated on the hair being lit on fire, Betty, but don't forget that Sam got pushed down his stairs, just like that guy in the band got pushed off the stage."

"Even if they do like revenge, we banished that demon. They can't come back." I looked at Maxwell. "Right?"

Maxwell hesitated. "Not that I know of. I've certainly never heard of it happening in the past."

"Maybe another demon is getting revenge on behalf of Sam's demon." Shaun just wasn't going to let his theory drop.

Again, though, Maxwell was hesitant. "If Sam's demon had been a flesh and blood entity, then I might agree. But all Sam had was a lesser demon without any real intelligence. It doesn't make sense that anyone would want to get revenge for a creature that carries little importance in demon hierarchy."

Shaun fell silent, though his face betrayed his reluctance to discount the demons. I sipped at my tea, my eyes staring at the wall in front of me. There were so many questions and theories running through my mind that I doubted I would be able to fall asleep at all that night.

Maxwell took my hand and raised it to his lips. He began to softly kiss each of the scratch marks, and I felt the tension in my shoulders fade. I turned to face him, and Maxwell's blue eyes conveyed his concern for me. "I'm sorry," he whispered.

Maxwell blamed himself for all of this. Granted, I wouldn't be in this situation if I'd never started dating him, but I didn't want Maxwell to feel guilty. I needed him to be strong if I was ever going to survive this, and there was no room for guilt.

Telling him not to feel that way wouldn't make any difference, though.

I squeezed Maxwell's hand. "Time for bed," I

announced. I still wasn't sleepy, but right now all I wanted to do was lie quietly next to Maxwell. It wouldn't stop my brain from running at full throttle, and it wouldn't keep me from worrying about what would happen to us next, but I needed the comfort of his body next to mine.

Maxwell seemed to understand without a single word from me. He immediately pulled me into his arms after we climbed in bed. One hand stroked my hair while the other trailed slowly across my skin. I shifted against him and could feel that danger and uncertainty weren't enough to keep him from still wanting me.

I raised my head and found Maxwell's lips, kissing him deeply. It seemed to take him by surprise, but he returned the kiss with equal passion. His hands began to explore further, and I slid my own hands down his body so I could guide him into me.

Maxwell's heat pulsed through my body with every thrust, and I saw the now-familiar red hue that tinted my vision whenever Maxwell and I were together. We climaxed at the same time, and I forgot about everything else as an intense heat radiated through me. All I knew for a few moments was the heat and Maxwell's body pressed tightly against mine, his lips forming my name against my ear.

Afterward, I easily fell asleep, my body once again cradled in Maxwell's arms.

I only woke up once during the night. I didn't know what brought me out of sleep, but I saw nothing in the darkness. There was a quiet pop. Maxwell must be keeping watch, and he had either just arrived from scouting outside the house, or he had just left. His movements must have been what woke me.

Except when I rolled over toward Maxwell's side of the bed, my hand found his shoulder. He was sound asleep.

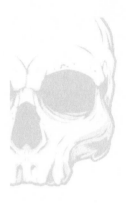

NINE

I leaped out of bed toward the light switch, turning around to face the room as light flooded it. There was no one there. Maxwell stirred and rolled over, and he was alert as soon as he saw my stance.

"There was a demon here," I said, explaining the noise I'd heard of a demon materializing.

Maxwell shook his head. "I think I would have sensed it."

"You were asleep."

"Everything looks like it's in order." Maxwell got up and made a quick search through his belongings, instructing me to do the same. When he was done, he spread his hands in defeat. "Nothing has been taken, and we haven't been hurt. Maybe you dreamed the sound?"

"No. Something woke me up, and I had opened my eyes already when I heard it."

"Come back to bed. I'll stay awake until morning." Maxwell pulled on his clothes before he got back into bed with me. Apparently he didn't like the idea of fighting a demon intruder naked. I also knew that he would be materializing outside, as he had been doing on previous nights.

"I don't like this," I said quietly. "It was bad enough when we only had to worry about the hunters, but now it seems like everyone is after us. I wish the demons and the demon hunters would just go back to fighting each other."

"I don't like it, either." Maxwell's tone lightened. "At least he didn't materialize here earlier and catch us having sex."

That thought, at least, made me laugh. It took a long time for me to fall asleep again. We left the light on, but eventually I dozed off once more. I didn't wake up again until the smell of blueberry muffins filled my nostrils. I opened my eyes, saw daylight streaming through the window, and realized that I was absolutely starving.

Maxwell and I didn't mention our late-night visitor to Shaun and Daisy. We never even discussed it with each other; we just both stayed quiet about it over breakfast. We should have told them: it was their house, and they had every right to know what was going on. Still, as Maxwell had pointed out, nothing bad had happened, and I didn't want to worry them needlessly.

It was December thirty-first, the last day of the year, and we had the New Year's Eve party at The Hex to look forward to. At least, I was trying to look forward to an evening in a bar haunted by an angry ghost.

Maxwell refused to go to a party wearing Shaun's clothes. Instead, he insisted on going shopping. He and Shaun went together, and I wasn't surprised when Maxwell came home with three new suits. He was going to be the best-dressed guy at the bar. Maxwell hadn't forgotten me, either. He had picked up several pairs of jeans, a basic black dress, and a big bag full of the laciest, sexiest lingerie he could find. I blushed just looking inside the bag. "I hope I got your size right. You can model it for me later," Maxwell said, winking.

Even though I expected it was futile, I decided to listen to our recordings from the night before. There was no point in reporting anything to Carlo, but I still hoped I might find some answers for myself.

Surprisingly, I did have one EVP. My new friend in the basement had spoken to us while we had heard the creaks on the stairs. Instead of answering our questions, though, I simply heard a man's rough voice say, "Cast out." The words were clear, but their meaning was not. Had the ghost been cast out of society when he was alive? Maybe his spirit was angry because of how others had treated him. Or, I mused, maybe he had been cast out after becoming a ghost. But cast out by whom and for what?

Carter called later with two pieces of news. First, he proudly told me that The Hex would allow Mick and Dwayne to bring their cameras to the party. "We won't have to wear our mics," Carter assured me. "They just want footage of us having fun for a change."

"Let's hope it is fun," I said.

Carter's other news was a lot more welcome to me. He had also caught an EVP. While Carter and I were upstairs in Carlo's bedroom, we got an EVP just before Carter had started choking. It was a high female voice that said, "Hurt, hurt." Each word was enunciated firmly, almost like a chant. It was a good catch, but didn't tell us anything.

"I'm used to getting cryptic EVPs," I said, "but this just doesn't seem fair. No one wants to talk. It's like the ghosts are so angry that all they can do is lash out."

"They're in a rage," Carter agreed.

———

I tried not to think about angry ghosts when we arrived at The Hex that night. I chose to wear a pair of my new jeans with a green silk blouse of Daisy's. It was casual enough for a bar, but I still looked nice. Of course, Maxwell outdid us all, wearing a three-piece black suit with a black shirt. "I know it's overkill," he told me, "but I haven't felt well-dressed for a week now."

Our names were on a list at the door, so I felt somewhat like a celebrity as I walked inside. It was already ten o'clock, and it was so crowded that I didn't know how we'd ever make it beyond the front door. Maxwell took the lead, guiding us to an open area between the door and the bar. A rock band was playing, making it hard to hear Daisy as she gestured toward the stage.

If I had felt like a celebrity, then Carter certainly acted like one. He arrived just a few minutes after us, striding through the door wearing a gray suit and sunglasses. Mick and Dwayne followed, their cameras rolling. Everyone Carter passed turned to stare, and I could only shake my head at his pretentious behavior.

Carter paused when he reached us, taking off his sunglasses before smirking and nodding in greeting. Without a word, he turned on his heel and headed for the bar. It was only then that I noticed Kayce following in Carter's wake. She was wearing a red dress that was so low cut that I worried she might fall out of it at any moment. Her blonde hair was teased to an impressive height, and a rhinestone barrette held the whole creation in place.

She should be using the barrette to hold her dress in place, I thought.

I looked at Daisy and rolled my eyes, but Daisy only giggled. "Is that the psychic?" Daisy leaned in so she could shout in my ear, and she said "psychic" like it was a vulgar word.

When I nodded, Daisy smiled wickedly. I had a feeling that she was going to put Kayce's claims to the test.

Carter and Kayce eventually rejoined us, each with a drink in hand, and Carter made a beeline for me. "Annie wants to see us in the office," he said. "All of us."

I motioned for Carter to lead the way, and I was

relieved when Shaun shut the door to the office, blocking out much of the noise. Annie was perched on the edge of her desk, her long legs stretched over the back of a chair. She was trying to look casual, but I could see the way her eyes narrowed when we walked in.

"Things are not getting better," she said after a precursory greeting. "In fact, they've gotten worse."

"Tell us," I said.

In answer, Annie pulled up the sleeve of her purple dress. Her upper arm was wrapped in gauze. "Apparently it was my turn to be attacked. Things settled down over the past couple of days, but this afternoon things started happening again. I was getting the bands settled in when something hit me in the arm. It was one of the knives we keep on the bar for slicing up limes. I bled all over the place."

None of us responded, and after looking around at our grim faces, Annie continued. "The second band that was supposed to play tonight cancelled. They were our headliner, too. The drummer went in the bathroom, and we all heard this loud bang. The other guys in the band ran in there and found him unconscious on the floor. He was bleeding so badly from his head that they had to take him to the hospital. When he woke up, he said that he'd been standing at the sink when something grabbed him from behind and slammed his head into the mirror."

Annie paused and looked wistfully in the direction of the bathrooms. "And they say it's seven years of bad luck if you break a mirror."

I sighed. I had thought the ghost here was trying to lash out against me somehow. After all, I was the only one who had been called by name, and hair getting lit on fire was far too much to be coincidence. This, though, made me think otherwise. Why was the ghost attacking people randomly?

I was wracking my brain for an answer when Carter spoke up. "Kayce here is a psychic. Maybe she can get some answers."

I pursed my lips, forcing myself to remain silent. I still wasn't convinced that Kayce had any psychic abilities, and I didn't want to look like an idiot if we paraded a fraud in front of one of our clients. Saying so would make me look just as bad, so I made a mental note to have a long conversation with Carter when I could get him alone. Then again, I might skip having a conversation in favor of just yelling at him.

Carter's suggestion angered me, but Annie perked up. "Really? My aunt had some of that intuition, but I don't. I'd love it if you could try to find out what's going on." Annie stretched out her hand to Kayce and introduced herself before turning to me. "Betty, I didn't know you had a psychic."

"I don't." To soften my response, I added, "Kayce is a friend of Carter's. The rest of us just met her a few days ago."

Gosh, had it really only been a few days? It had been one hell of a week.

"The band plays for another forty minutes," Annie said. "I'll take you in the green room now, while it's empty."

The two of them left with Carter following eagerly behind. Mick and Dwayne had been waiting in the hallway —the office was too small for everyone to fit—and Carter gestured excitedly to them to follow.

"Good riddance," Daisy said after they left. "Carter is showing her off like a new puppy."

"I just hope she doesn't make us all look foolish," I said.

"Cheer up, Betty. She is Carter's friend, so she'll only

make him look foolish. On TV, no less." Daisy looked immensely pleased at the idea.

"Daisy's just jealous that someone has better intuition than her," Shaun said, playfully poking Daisy's growing belly.

"All of you are welcome to stay in here and talk about psychics all night," Maxwell said, "but I'm going to go out there and enjoy my New Year's Eve." He offered his arm to me, and I gladly took it. We lucked out and found two empty seats at the bar: one for me and one for Daisy. Maxwell draped one arm casually across my shoulders, and I had to hide a smile when I noticed how many women gave me dirty looks. Jealousy was not pretty. Every woman seemed interested in Maxwell, and a college-aged girl boldly elbowed her way between Daisy and me so she could lean against the bar. She popped one hip toward Maxwell and eyed him over her shoulder.

Maxwell leaned over me and put his lips against my neck. To the girl, it looked like he was kissing the skin just below my ear. What he was really doing was hiding his smile. When the girl realized she wasn't going to get any positive response from Maxwell—or a negative one from me—she threw her money on the bar, grabbed her drink, and stomped off in a huff. As soon as she was gone, all four of us burst out laughing.

When a glass shattered against the back of the bar just a few seconds later, I thought for sure that the girl had thrown her drink at us. The bartender, though, was staring at a rack of glasses sitting next to the sink. "Did you see that?" he asked. "It just popped right out of there and slammed against the bar!"

The ghost was being bold, causing activity where hundreds of people might witness it. If anything else happened, and if enough people saw it, it could create a panic. The last thing we needed was a bar full of people stampeding toward the front door to escape a ghost.

"We need to make this ghost calm down," I said to Daisy. "Any ideas?"

"Maybe we should leave," she said hesitantly.

"I don't think we're the problem. This started before we arrived."

"I think we should dance," Maxwell said suddenly. He grabbed my hand and pulled me up, leading me toward the floor. I realized that the band was playing a slow rock ballad, and other couples were dancing, too.

Maxwell pulled me into his arms and began to sway gracefully to the music. It was the first time we had danced together, and I wasn't surprised to find that he was good at it. Maxwell was good at just about everything because he'd had so many years to hone his skills.

"I don't think leaving would help things, but I also think this is tied to you, somehow," Maxwell said into my ear.

"I don't know if I think that anymore," I said. "People completely unconnected with me are being attacked."

"And you keep winding up right in the middle of it."

"Well, yeah," I conceded, "but I'm a ghost hunter. That's kind of how it works."

Maxwell pulled back so we were eye-to-eye. He gazed at me for a long time before he leaned in and kissed me. "If anything else happens tonight, we are going to leave. I won't risk your safety."

I just sighed and rested my head on Maxwell's shoulder. I would gladly leave, as long as I could finish this dance with him.

When the song ended, the band broke into another up-tempo song. Maxwell and I were close to the stage, so we turned and watched them play a couple of songs. They were loud, but good. While we stood there, a man brushed against me as he passed, balancing three cups of beer. His arm was hot against mine, and I was reminded of my first impression of Carlo. I felt my breath catch in my throat.

You're being silly, I told myself. We're in the middle of a crowded bar; of course that guy's skin is hot.

Still, I took Maxwell's hand and held tightly, noticing that his temperature felt the same as that of the man who had passed me.

After someone else nearly tipped their drink onto me, we returned to the bar, where Daisy was happily sipping a ginger ale. The band wrapped up, and there was instantly a crush of people at the bar, all clamoring for drinks. A tall man with a mohawk squeezed in next to me and shouted for a shot of whiskey. "You want one?" he said, turning to me.

"No, thanks," I said.

He shrugged. "Your loss." When the bartender put the shot down in front of him, the man downed it immediately. As he turned away, he put his hand on my arm. "Happy New Year!"

I shrank back from his touch. It was just as hot as Maxwell's and the other man's. What was going on? I felt my chest tighten as I began to worry that there were demons all around me. Here I had been worried that the ghost's antics would create panic, and I was getting panicky about a couple of men with a lot of body heat. Maxwell looked unconcerned, though, so I knew I was just being paranoid. I needed to get my fear under control so I could actually enjoy my evening.

I excused myself and hurried to the bathroom. When I got in a stall, I leaned my forehead against the door and took a few deep breaths. Several girls at the sinks were complaining about how much their boyfriends were drinking, and I wished that my biggest care in life was how big the bar tab would be. I didn't want to think about living in this kind of fear and nervous anticipation for the rest of my life.

When I felt like I had myself under control again, I left the bathroom. I squeezed past a group of girls talking in the hallway and ran right into someone. I was already apologizing when I recognized the long, lank hair hanging down past his shoulders.

"Lou!"

Lou's eyes widened like a cornered animal. "Betty!" Lou's eyes darted from side to side, looking for an escape.

"What are you doing here?"

"I just...um...it's New Year's." Lou ran a hand nervously along his jawline. Lou hadn't shaved in a while, and he looked a little rough. He had never been a neat freak when it came to his appearance, but now his face bordered on haggard.

It wasn't fair of me to be suspicious of running into Lou here. I knew he had been to The Hex in the past, and tonight's band played the type of music he loved. Still, nothing in my life lately had happened just by coincidence. In an effort to be somewhat civil, I said, "Thank you for coming to my rescue the other night."

"Oh, that." Lou was still looking at everything except me. He shifted uncomfortably. "I'm sorry about that. He wasn't supposed to attack you."

"Lou, I appreciate the fact that you don't want me to get hurt, but I don't think the other hunters share your sentiment. They think I'm every bit as evil as Maxwell, and whatever they may be telling you, not one of them cares if I live or die."

Lou was shaking his head. "No, we have an understanding. They aren't going to do anything to you."

"They already have. Just knowing they're after us is driving me mad. I've been living in fear for weeks now."

"Fear of what?" Lou seemed genuinely curious.

"Fear that they're going to retaliate. It's not a question of if, it's a question of when. I know it's coming, and just turning a corner on the street is terrifying for me. I'm practically under house arrest right now!"

Lou finally looked me in the eye. "I know it's hard to believe, considering what happened at Maxwell's house, but they are not going to harm you. You know there are hunters here in Savannah. Have they attacked you or caused you any harm at all?"

"Yes, that guy…"

"Other than him," Lou interrupted.

"Other than the guy in the alley, no. I haven't been attacked."

"And no demon hunter is going to attack you in the future, either. I promise." Lou glanced quickly behind him. "I gotta go," he mumbled.

"Don't feel like you have to leave because of me."

"It's not you." Lou pushed past me without another word. I stood and watched as he slipped out the back door.

That was the longest conversation that Lou and I had had in two months. It left me feeling melancholy. Lou and I had once been good friends, and now he could barely even meet my eye. We weren't friends anymore, but I did appreciate that Lou still didn't want me to get hurt. He very much wanted Maxwell to be banished to hell, and he wasn't afraid to use me to make that happen, but he still had a shred of humanity left.

There was hope for Lou, after all.

I wandered back toward the bar, but before I could get there, the tall man with the mohawk stopped me. "You're the ghost hunter, right? Your hot friend is looking for you."

At my blank stare, he clarified. "Blonde, leggy, nice curves."

"Oh. Thanks for letting me know."

I only had a moment to wonder why Kayce was trying

to find me when Mohawk took me by the elbow. "She's back by the sound booth. I'll show you."

Mohawk propelled me along even as I tried to make my excuses. I passed within ten feet of Maxwell, Shaun, and Daisy, but it was so crowded that I couldn't even see them.

As we neared the back of the bar, Mohawk stopped. "Well, she was here a minute ago. Guess she got tired of waiting." He turned to me and grinned.

"Thanks, anyway," I said. Mohawk's lopsided smile was unnerving, but that wasn't enough reason for me to be impolite. I turned to walk back to the bar, but his grip tightened on my elbow. As it did, I felt a searing heat against my skin. It radiated up my arm and down into my hand.

I hadn't been acting silly earlier, after all. Mohawk was a demon.

I looked up and saw that the man who'd passed me earlier, bumping against me with his hot skin, was now standing in front of us. He wore an eager grin, as well.

To my right, two more men emerged from the crowd. I couldn't see over Mohawk's shoulder, but I knew I was surrounded by demons.

In unison, they stepped forward and each laid one hand on me. Every place they were touching me began to burn. My arms were pinned to my sides. I opened my mouth to scream, but Mohawk leaned in and pressed his lips hard against mine. I tried to turn my head away, but Mohawk gripped the back of my head with his free hand. I couldn't move, and the music was too loud for anyone to hear my muffled cries.

The demons were going to kill me, right in front of hundreds of New Year's Eve revelers. They formed such a tight circle around me that I doubted anyone would notice when my body turned to ash, incinerated by the demons.

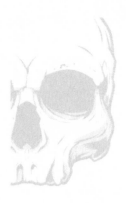

TEN

My vision began to blur, and Mohawk's face appeared red. The heat from his lips sent a burning sensation down my throat. I breathed through my nose, but the air was hot by the time it reached my lungs.

More hands grabbed me when my knees gave out. I was in agonizing pain. I had felt this sensation before, but only from one demon. Now, it came from many, and I knew it wouldn't take long before their combined efforts were too much for my body to bear.

I shut my eyes, but still I saw red flashes pulsing against my eyelids. I didn't hear the music anymore, and I forgot that I was still standing with demons supporting me. My mind focused solely on the shifting red as I began to lose consciousness.

Even as I slipped away, I felt a rush of cool air against my face. Mohawk was no longer kissing me, and his hand slid quickly from my head. The other hands began to let go of me, too, and without their support, I felt my body slumping to the floor. Before I reached it, someone caught me.

I was picked up like a new bride being carried over the threshold, and I felt my feet knocking against people as I was carried somewhere. I breathed in the comparatively cool air of the bar, and as my mind became aware again, I noticed that the hands holding me were warm. Maxwell must have come to my rescue. Without opening my eyes, I slid my arms around his shoulders.

"Sorry, my girl here had a little too much to drink," he said to someone we passed. Except it wasn't Maxwell's voice. It was deeper and accented. I cracked one eye open. Carlo was carrying me toward the back hallway, where I had run into Lou.

I had been rescued from a pack of demons only to be abducted by another.

My efforts to struggle against Carlo were weak, and he laughed softly. "Calm down, Betty. You're safe."

Carlo walked down the hall and right out the back door. When we were in the alley behind the bar, he put me down gently. "Are you okay to stand?"

My knees were shaking, but I didn't want to lean on Carlo for support. "I'm fine."

"No, you're not. You were one minute away from death in there."

I sat down on a pile of crates stacked by the door. My knees weren't the only things that were shaking. My hands shook so badly that I slid them under my thighs and sat on them. "Why are you trying to kill me?"

"I am not trying to kill you, as you can see."

"Then why were all those other demons trying to?"

Carlo sighed and sat down next to me. He pulled out a cigarette, lit it, and took a long drag before he answered. "They have their reasons. It is not for me to talk about demon business with mortals. I will tell you this, though. I was on their side until recently."

"You wanted me dead? Why?"

"Because I would have received a great reward for killing you." Carlo looked surprised that he was willingly giving up his reward by letting me live.

"A reward from…?" I prompted.

Carlo raised a warning finger. "I have said enough. Again, demon business is between demons and our boss."

"Satan."

"Yes."

I wanted to ask why hell had a reward out for my death. And how did all of those demons even find out? Was there some sort of demonic e-newsletter that they all received? I felt like a mouse being pursued by a pack of cats. Carlo's lips were set firmly, though, and I knew I wouldn't get any answers. Instead, I asked, "What made you change your mind about killing me?" I couldn't believe I was sitting in an alley with a demon, casually chatting about my hypothetical murder. My life had certainly changed a lot in recent weeks. I even found myself wondering just how much reward money I was worth.

"I have been working for someone my entire existence," Carlo said. "Recently, I have begun to question things. When I invited you to my house, Betty, I had every intention of letting my ghosts rip you to shreds. I thought it would be entertaining. Then I met you, and I realized that you are a good soul. I did not want that end for you."

Carlo had reconsidered, just as Maxwell had said he felt remorse for some of the people he had sent to hell over the years.

"I used to think that demons were the only evil in this world," Carlo continued. "Now I know that evil can come in many forms. It is time for me to reconsider where I stand and who I work for."

Carlo stood and gestured toward the door. "They will not come out here, not while I'm with you. I'm older and have more authority than them, and they probably think I brought you here to kill you myself."

I held up a hand to stop Carlo. "My boyfriend," I began, "he's—"

"I know who and what Maxwell is," Carlo said when I

hesitated. "And no, they're not after him. There is only a reward for you. Stay close to him, Betty. The demons are not likely to attack you if you're with him."

I nodded grimly. I hadn't been imagining things when I'd heard that pop in our bedroom: a demon had materialized there, and the only reason I hadn't been attacked right there in bed was because of Maxwell's presence.

I texted Maxwell and told him to round everyone up as quickly as he could. Carlo stayed with me while I waited for them. "Thank you," I told him. "I realize I didn't have anything to do with you changing your mind, but I appreciate not being dead."

Carlo laughed softly. "You did have something to do with it. Had I met you and found you to be a bad person, or a lost soul, then I would not have hesitated to let Rebecca and Charles kill you."

"Rebecca and Charles?"

"Yes. My ghosts, of course. They are, ordinarily, very pleasant houseguests. They changed their appearance to be more frightening. They did an excellent job, don't you think?"

I was about to respond when the back door slammed open and I jumped, expecting a renewed attack. Instead, Maxwell strode out, followed closely by the rest of my friends. Maxwell's face contorted with anger when he saw Carlo. I stood up and planted myself between them. "Carlo just saved my life," I said quickly. Maxwell opened his mouth, but I put up a hand to stop him. "I will explain everything, but not here. We need to leave, now."

Carlo escorted us to Shaun's car, and Carter promised to follow us to the house. Mick and Dwayne were wide-eyed as they filmed every step we took. I was walking slowly, still hurting from the demon attack, and Carlo gave me a hand as I lowered myself into the back seat. "I have never had any regrets," he said. "I believe I would have if I had not met you. Thank you, Betty."

I thanked Carlo again for rescuing me, and I glanced back to see him dematerialize as Shaun pulled out of the parking lot. Everyone began asking questions at the same time.

Maxwell put his arm around my shoulders and drew me close to him. He kissed my temple and said, "I'm so sorry I wasn't there for you."

"It's okay. Who knew I could get into so much trouble just a couple dozen feet away from you?" I reached up and squeezed his hand reassuringly.

I haltingly described running into Lou and the demon attack. I was so exhausted after nearly being incinerated that it was hard to focus. Maxwell was especially curious about Carlo's information. He wanted to know why there was a reward for my death just as badly as I did.

"Why would Carlo's 'boss,' as he puts it, want me dead?" I asked.

"I'm not sure why. Unless, of course, it's just for sport."

I wrinkled my nose. "Does that happen?"

"Well, you're dating me, so it's likely that you have come to his attention. Look at the effort that Tage went through to try to win your soul for hell. Maybe this is some kind of game, and you're the prize."

I got chills at that thought. At least the demon hunters would only kill me. The demons would kill me and send me to hell. It wasn't an ending I could think about for any length of time without feeling sick to my stomach.

Carter and Kayce were already waiting for us at Shaun and Daisy's. Carter had talked Mick and Dwayne into calling it a night, but Carter looked ready for more excitement. I had to repeat my story for him and Kayce while Daisy gave me milk and graham crackers again. The night's events and the milk made me so sleepy that I barely heard Carter say, "Kayce has something really important to tell you." I tried to nod my head, but awareness slipped away as I did. I fell asleep right there at the kitchen table, and I didn't wake up until the next morning.

———

Every muscle in my body hurt when I woke up, and my throat ached. Even my lips felt chapped and raw. I rolled over but didn't open my eyes. There were a lot more questions that needed to be answered, and I didn't want to deal with any of them.

I felt someone sit down on the bed next to me, and then Maxwell's voice spoke quietly in my ear. "Happy New Year."

"I'm not sure what's so happy about it," I mumbled.

"You're still alive."

I groaned in response. I hurt so badly that I wasn't sure being alive was the better option at the moment.

"And Daisy made waffles," Maxwell added.

I was willing to get out of bed for waffles, at least. Maxwell kept a steadying hand on my arm as I wobbled down the hallway to the kitchen. Someone—Maxwell, I assumed—had gotten me into pajamas the night before, and I didn't bother to put on real clothes. Waffles seemed more important than getting dressed.

I instantly regretted that decision when I walked into the kitchen and saw Mick, a camera already in his hand. Dwayne stood nearby with a stack of body mics in his hands. "Oh, crap," I said. I pivoted and walked right back out.

Fifteen minutes later, I returned, ready for both waffles and camera time. Daisy had already poured me a cup of coffee, which I gratefully accepted. Once I'd had a few sips, I pointed at Carter and Kayce. "What are you doing here?"

"Time for a group meeting," Carter said dryly. "Daisy insisted after you got attacked. We have to decide how we're going to deal with this."

"I'm still trying to get used to this whole concept of demons running around Savannah," Dwayne spoke up.

I looked at Carter, one eyebrow raised. "They needed to know, Betty. When I invited them here, I never expected that we'd wind up in this situation."

Carter was right. Even if he sent Mick and Dwayne home right now, they had a right to know how close to danger they had been. This was the second time we had put them in harm's way. I mulled that over as I chewed a big bite of waffle.

Everyone fell silent, something that almost never happened when Carter and Daisy were in the same room. I could feel everyone watching me, and I knew there was some bad news no one had told me yet. "Just say it, whatever it is," I said, putting down my fork.

"Kayce has something to tell you," Carter said.

I waved a hand at Kayce, inviting her to proceed.

"I communicated with the spirit at The Hex last night," Kayce began hesitantly.

"Would this be before or after a horde of demons attacked me?"

"Probably at the same time. Carter and I went to the green room. It was still loud in there, but we sat quietly so I could try to focus. I could feel the spirit, and it was incredibly angry. I sensed a lot of rage but also confusion. The spirit built up so much negative energy that the cameras wouldn't even work."

"Which means we missed out on some great footage of this girl doing her thing," Mick said.

"The spirit didn't even want to talk to me," Kayce

continued, "but I was persistent, and finally I started getting some impressions. Betty, you were right about these cases being tied to you."

I frowned. "You're saying that it is some kind of poltergeist activity? I thought we had discounted that theory."

"No, the cases aren't tied to you in that way. These spirits were told things about you. I don't know what, but I know it was things that really angered all of them. When you showed up to investigate, they knew who you were, and they lashed out."

"That doesn't explain why the ghosts were acting violently before I ever showed up to investigate," I pointed out.

"They were told to do that by the same people who turned them against you."

"And these people would be…?" I didn't really need to ask because I was pretty sure that I knew the answer already. Still, I couldn't bring myself to say it, so I needed someone else to voice the truth.

"It's the demon hunters, Betty," Carter said quietly. "They got these ghosts to stage violent activity, then made sure your team was recommended to the owners of the places being haunted."

I nodded slowly. "Daisy had pointed out that Annie called my cell the first time she contacted us, even though it's my home number listed on the website for The Seekers. I naturally assumed that someone had passed my name and number on to her, though I never suspected it was a demon hunter."

"It seems that the spirits were instructed to harm you," Kayce said. "I got the impression that the hunters wanted to have you killed, but the spirit at The Hex seemed reluctant about going that far. He just wanted to hurt you and scare you. Carter, too, from what I understood."

"Lou," I said suddenly.

"What about him?" Shaun asked.

"When I ran into him last night, I told him that I'd been living in terror because I didn't know when the hunters were going to attack. He promised me that they weren't going to hurt me. He even went so far as to imply that I was being needlessly cautious because none of them had hurt me yet."

"Except for that jerk at Maxwell's house," Daisy said.

"Believe me, I pointed that out, too. The hunters might have agreed not to hurt me in order to placate Lou, but they didn't agree not to get someone—or something—else to hurt me. They're trying to use ghosts so they won't have to claim responsibility for anything that happens to me."

It seemed like the perfect explanation until Daisy said, "Or maybe Lou knows exactly what they're doing because he orchestrated it."

I did not like that option at all. I wanted to believe that Lou still had some concern for my welfare, but I had to concede that Daisy had a point when she continued, "Think about it, Betty. The last three investigations have involved elements from past ones: hair getting lit on fire, your name on the wall, the revenants. Lou was there for all of that. None of the other hunters would have known those kinds of details, and they certainly wouldn't have known how much reenacting those things would bother you."

The only response I could muster was a string of expletives. Lou had lied about not wanting any harm to come to me. He had looked me in the eye, and he had lied.

I started crying right there in front of everyone.

Maxwell's arms were around me in an instant, and he ordered Mick to turn off his camera. I felt the sting of losing Lou's friendship all over again, and this time I knew that, no matter what, we would never be on good terms with each other. I had wanted so badly to believe that there was some part of him that still cared about me, but now I knew that he was utterly against me. Lou was willing to lead me into a false sense of security even while he worked to bring danger or even death right to me.

And what, I wondered, would happen if our roles were reversed? Would I ever willingly put Lou in harm's way? Would I kill him in order to eliminate an enemy? I hoped that I would never do such a thing, and I really hoped that my resolve would never be put to the test.

I was mopey for the rest of the morning. I had thought that living in fear of the demon hunters was as bad as it got. Then I'd added violent ghosts to that list. After last night, I was currently avoiding demon hunters, ghosts, and demons. That was bad enough. But this disappointment I felt about Lou trumped all of my other emotions. Maxwell and Daisy positioned themselves on either side of me as I sat on the couch. Daisy had put a copy of *Bedknobs and Broomsticks* in the DVD player, but I hardly noticed. I was, however, infinitely grateful to have her and Maxwell with me. I didn't know if I could ever convey to them how much comfort their presence gave me.

Carter took Kayce home before going back to his house with Mick and Dwayne. It was nice to have fewer people staring at me, but I was worried about Carter's safety. He had been attacked by the female ghost at Carlo's house, so I knew he was in just as much danger as I was. I had offended the hunters more by killing one of their own, but Carter was their enemy just the same.

I was still sitting on the couch at two o'clock in the afternoon when my phone rang. It was Annie at The Hex, and she sounded more perturbed than scared. "This ghost is really out of control," she shouted.

"There has been more violence?" I asked. I would have to find some way of telling Annie that her ghost was acting up because someone had angered it, and I hoped I could do it without mentioning my involvement.

"What's that? I can't hear you." Annie was still shouting, and I wondered if a band was doing a sound check. I could hear a vague high-pitched noise that might be a guitar.

I repeated my question loudly, and Annie laughed mirthlessly when she finally understood me. "No, but I wish that was all the ghost was doing," she said. "It's wailing like a damn banshee, and it's been going non-stop since I got here an hour ago."

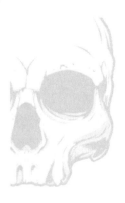

ELEVEN

Annie hadn't been lying about the ghost wailing like a banshee. I could hear the high-pitched scream on the sidewalk outside The Hex. Inside, frustrated bartenders tried to prepare for that night's crowd while their ears were inundated with the noise. It changed pitch and intensity, but rarely paused.

"This is awful," Kayce shouted at me. I'd called Carter as soon as I'd gotten off the phone with Annie, and I had actually asked him to bring Kayce. After last night, I had little doubt that she really did have some kind of psychic ability. Even Daisy, who had stayed at home, had to agree begrudgingly that Kayce was a real, honest-to-goodness psychic medium.

There was a clatter behind me as I passed the bar to Annie's office. When I turned, I saw Mick and Dwayne standing with their hands clamped over their ears. They had walked in with their headphones on so they could hear the audio feed from their cameras. They had ripped the headphones off and thrown them down: the wailing had been amplified by their equipment.

"It's all right," Dwayne said. "I just might be deaf for a day or two."

The only one who didn't seem at all affected by the

noise was Maxwell, who moved easily, not wincing like the rest of us.

Annie was in her office, staring at spreadsheets on her computer screen but not getting anything done. "I just can't concentrate with this noise," she said.

"Any idea what's causing it?" I was going to be hoarse if I had to shout the whole time we were here.

Annie shook her head. "Not a clue. I hope you brought your equipment."

"Even better. We brought our psychic." Carter said, looking at Kayce proudly. With her good looks and Carter's obvious admiration of her, I had a feeling I'd been supplanted as Carter's "sidekick" for investigations.

Before Carter spilled all of the details about Kayce's discovery the night before, I jumped in and gave Annie a brief description. I left out mention of myself or Carter, saying only that the ghost seemed really angry and that we hoped to curb its anger by communicating with it through Kayce.

"Good luck," Annie said. "We'll be setting up, but go anywhere you like. We don't open for another couple of hours, so take your time."

Like Annie and her spreadsheets, I didn't know how Kayce was going to concentrate enough to even make the initial contact with the ghost. She chose to sit in the green room again, though the wailing was just as bad in there. The noise didn't seem to stem from any one point. It was just everywhere at once, no quieter or louder anywhere we went.

Kayce sat on her knees in the center of the floor. Carter kneeled down close to her side, while Shaun, Maxwell, and I stood in a loose arc behind her. Mick and Dwayne took up positions on opposite ends of the room. It was cramped with all of us in there.

I put my hands over my ears and shut my eyes. The

wailing seemed to be in my head now, not just in the air around me. I wondered if anyone else felt that way.

Kayce bowed her head. I couldn't tell if she was speaking out loud to the ghost or not since I was behind her, but after a few moments her head snapped up. "I said yes!" she shouted. Even with the ghost's wails and my hands over my ears, I could hear Kayce loudly.

And then, just like that, the wailing ceased. The sudden silence was startling. Kayce let out a big breath and said, "Finally. I asked it to stop so we could communicate, and it wanted to know if we were going to help."

"I'm not sure we came here to help, necessarily," I said carefully. "We're trying to get some answers."

A floor lamp in one corner fell over in response. I raised my hands in surrender. "But if we can help you in any way, we would certainly be happy to," I added.

"Now," Kayce instructed, "I need each of you to focus your thoughts on the spirit. Make sure they are positive thoughts." Kayce craned her head around and peered up at me.

"What? You don't have to worry about me. This is the same ghost that lobbed things at my head. I don't want to anger it any more."

Kayce just narrowed her eyes at me before returning her gaze to the wall in front of her. "Concentrate, now," she said. Kayce's head bowed again, and she didn't move for several minutes at least. The only change I saw was her breathing, which became deep and labored, like she was struggling for air.

I was actually getting a little bored. Watching a psychic in action was not as exciting as they made it seem on TV. Too bad this investigation doesn't have tight editing and a dramatic soundtrack, I thought wryly. Then I remembered Mick and Dwayne and realized that, by the time anyone outside this room saw the investigation, it would have those things.

My wandering thoughts were interrupted when Kayce let out an exasperated, "Come on!"

"I thought the ghost was going to cooperate?" Shaun asked.

"He just keeps saying the same word over and over: demons." Kayce stood and put her hands on her hips. "If he wants us to help, he's going to have to tell us more than that."

"He could be referring to the demons that were here last night," Maxwell said. "The ghost might feel like they have invaded his haunt, and he wants help ensuring they don't come back."

"I tried asking if that's what he wants, but he wouldn't answer." Kayce looked at Dwayne and his camera self-consciously.

"Let me try," Maxwell said. "We know it doesn't like me, but if its problem is with demons, then I might be able to get somewhere."

Maxwell moved in front of Kayce so that he was at the center of the group. He stood erect, his jaw jutting forward defiantly. "You don't like me, I know, but we have a common enemy," he began, speaking with a firm confidence. "I don't like the demons who were here last night any more than you do. In fact, I probably hate them even more. They tried to kill my girlfriend."

I jumped as a voice whispered in my ear, "Betty." I whirled around, but of course no one was there.

"He just said my name," I said quietly. Maybe Maxwell would actually get somewhere by speaking with the entity, demon to ghost.

"That's right, Betty is the one they attacked," Maxwell continued. "Your anger with her is unfounded. Perhaps we could make a deal: if you forgive Betty and stop hurting

114

her and others, we promise to make sure that no demon ever steps foot in here again."

Maxwell paused, then added, "You have my word."

Kayce had taken a step away from Maxwell—I think she was still reconciling with the fact that not only did demons take corporeal form, but she was investigating with one—but now she stepped forward and laid a hand on his shoulder. "He doesn't trust you," she said. "I don't think giving your word means much to him."

"It was worth a try." Maxwell returned to me and said under his breath, "Carter's camera boys are going to have to be very selective with which footage they turn in." I nodded. It would be dangerous if people knew what Maxwell was and, more than that, I figured that most viewers of the show would just think he was nuts for claiming to be a demon.

All we had managed to accomplish so far was that we had gotten the ghost to quiet down. He was, apparently, still angry and very, very stubborn.

"We could try another EVP session," Carter suggested. "Now that it's quiet in here, we might have a chance of actually getting something."

"Actually, there's something I'd like to try," Kayce spoke up. "It's not something I've ever done before, but I've seen it done by other psychics." She was looking again at Dwayne, and I knew she wanted another chance to produce something good for the cameras. Kayce's reasons for wanting to try a new approach were self-serving, but I was happy to play along if there was any chance of getting some answers about the ghost's distress.

Mick jumped in front of Kayce, focusing his camera on her. "First, tell me what you're going to do," he instructed.

Kayce complied, sounding like an infomercial as she outlined her plan. "Betty has said that the demon hunters have put her in danger more than once. If I can channel her memories to the ghost, then maybe he'll understand that he's on the wrong side. He's been deceived by the demon hunters, and he needs to know it so he can calm down and stop causing harm."

It sounded incredibly far-fetched to me, but I was willing to try pretty much anything. Kayce made me sit down on the floor, and she sat directly in front of me, our faces nearly touching. Her proximity was uncomfortable, but I figured it would help her tap into my memories.

"You'll have to concentrate very hard, Betty," Kayce said. "Pick one memory of the demon hunters putting you in danger and focus on that. I want you to feel it as deeply as you can. Focus. Focus, focus, focus."

I gave Kayce a curt nod and shut my eyes. Her hands cupped either side of my face, and her forehead pressed against mine. I struggled to stay still, willing myself to concentrate on a memory rather than the feeling of her face against mine.

I thought of Joseph Stryker shooting me, grazing my thigh on purpose. He had wanted me to be in danger and helpless, but not dead. I thought of my surprise when I had heard the gunshot, the pain, the blood blossoming across my jeans, and the bang as the door of the barn Carter and I were trapped in had been shut and locked.

I went over the scenario again and again, remembering more detail each time. Kayce squeezed my face with her hands. "Concentrate, Betty. Make it stronger. I can't feel anything from you yet."

My mind suddenly landed on a different memory. I vividly saw Rob Sanders, Joseph's partner, inches away from me, just as Kayce was. I felt the heaviness of Rob's pudgy body pressing mine down on the bed, and I saw the beads of sweat on his shiny forehead. His glasses slid slowly down his nose as his perspiration worsened. My body jerked as I remembered Rob's knife sinking into my side, the blade sending a screaming pain through my chest and into my head.

This time, the memory wasn't a scene that ran through my head. It was one perfect picture of fear and pain. My heartbeat was rapid, and I didn't know if it was really speeding up or if it was just the memory of how hard it had beat the night Rob threatened me. As I mentally stared at the image of that moment, I felt a growing tension, like a rubber band stretched almost to the point of snapping.

There was a feminine shout, and I frowned. That hadn't been a part of the memory. I tentatively opened one eye and saw Kayce sprawled backwards on the floor.

Carter was already bending down to help her up, and Kayce rubbed the back of her head. When she looked up at me, I saw that she had tears in her eyes. "What happened next? Did he…?"

"Maxwell came to my rescue. I didn't know it at the time. I thought a ghost had jumped in to defend me." I raised a hand to my forehead and realized that I was sweating.

"Carter said they had mistreated you, but that was worse than I'd imagined." Kayce was actually smiling now. "It was exactly what we needed. The ghost got that message loud and clear, I promise you."

"Let's just hope that it sways him to forgive and forget," Maxwell said. He crouched down and put his hands on my shoulders. "You okay?"

"Yeah. It's just not a night I like to think about."

"Me, neither."

Maxwell moved to help me up, but I waved him off. "I think I need to sit for a minute. I feel exhausted."

"Because I was pulling energy from you along with your memory," Kayce said. Her tone was very matter-of-fact.

"How come you fell over?" I said. If she was pulling energy from me, then she should have been able to stay upright. Maybe Mick or Dwayne could give me a peek at that footage. It would be fun to watch.

"I was drawing energy from you to help boost the signal to the ghost, but suddenly you just smacked me with a huge wave of it," Kayce said. "It was like you had reached your limit and just...pow!" Kayce mimed a right hook.

I opened my mouth to apologize, but Kayce hadn't hesitated to suck my energy away in the first place. If she got an extra dose of it, then fine. I mentally chastised myself. It really wasn't fair of me to think like that about her. We had gotten off to a rocky start—she did accuse me of being the cause of these hauntings, after all—but she was proving to be useful. Not only that, but she seemed eager to help. I should have been thanking Kayce with all my heart, but instead I still felt a slight hesitation about her. She might be a real psychic, but there was still something about her that felt fake.

Maybe it was the wide-eyed look she was giving Mick's camera, talking about how my energy had given her a mental punch. I just rolled my eyes.

When Kayce finally turned away from the camera, I said, "You say the ghost got the message, so what now?"

"Now we find out if he's going to realize that his anger was misguided." Kayce glanced at Mick. "It's all up to me, now."

I turned slowly to Carter and raised my eyebrows. Somehow, against all the odds, he had found a woman who had as much ego as he did. I wasn't even sure how it was possible for the two of them to exist in the same room together. There just wasn't enough room for so much self-assurance.

Kayce sat on the floor again after shooing me to the

side. I was too tired to stand yet, so I scooted over and leaned gratefully against Maxwell's legs. Kayce shut her eyes and bowed her head again. A few seconds later, the wailing started up with renewed force.

"What did you say to it?" I shouted, covering my ears again.

Kayce didn't answer. Her brow furrowed in concentration, and she leaned so far forward that I thought she might roll right over.

Gradually, the wailing began to slow. It became a low moan, then disappeared altogether. Kayce's stance hadn't changed, and we sat silently, waiting for her to finish whatever she was doing.

My right side became cold, and the gravelly voice of the ghost whispered, "Sorry."

"It's okay," I murmured.

The cold dissolved, and Maxwell shifted behind me. "The ghost has moved to another part of the building," he announced. "I think he's finished listening to our case."

Kayce opened her eyes then, nodding slowly like she was coming out of a deep sleep. "He's satisfied."

"Tell us what happened," Mick said, squatting down to frame Kayce in his camera lens.

Kayce blinked rapidly a few times, smiled, and looked up at the camera brightly. "I was successful. The ghost realized that Betty is the victim, not the demon hunters. He has promised to stop being violent, but in return he wants Maxwell to honor his promise that no demon will ever come here again."

Carter immediately launched into enthusiastic praise of Kayce's success. He had never complimented me that way. Instead, Carter had always found fault with my methods of investigating. In fact, I realized, I had never met anyone that Carter so wholeheartedly approved of. It was disconcerting, like I had stepped into a parallel universe that was just slightly askew from the normal world.

I was so absorbed in watching their exchange that I didn't realize Shaun was talking to me until he poked me with a finger. "Boo? You there?"

"Sorry, Shaun, what?"

"I was saying that we should tell Annie the news and get out of here. I don't expect the demons from last night to be hanging around the area, but the shorter our visit, the better."

"Right. Okay." Maxwell helped me up, and I walked slowly behind the others. I was the last one to leave the green room, and even though I knew the ghost had wandered elsewhere, I turned and said, "Thank you."

Annie was so ecstatic about our success that she hugged every one of us. She offered us free VIP status for life—no cover charge, ever—and a free round of drinks every time we came to The Hex. After what I'd been through in the past week, I was ready to take up her drink offer on the spot. I could do with a glass of wine. In fact, I felt I had earned it.

Instead, Shaun prodded us to say farewell and hit the road. Before we left, Maxwell told Annie to expect a visit from a priest. He was vague on the reason for the visit, and Annie assumed it was to keep her ghost subdued. Maxwell would have the club consecrated to keep the demons from returning, fulfilling his promise to the ghost. He assured me that it could be done without exorcising any resident ghosts, unlike what had happened to my apartment and Lieutenant Griffin.

I was cordial to Kayce as we parted, thanking her for her help. My New Year's resolution, I decided, was to give her a fair chance.

All too soon I was back at Daisy and Shaun's house, locked up like a prisoner again. I suggested that we go out to eat to celebrate, but I received a firm no from everyone. Maxwell was sympathetic, adding, "I'm pretty much stuck here, too. At least we're in it together."

"I know. I might go crazy if you weren't with me."

"Who's to say you're not crazy?" Daisy asked. "I've got a pitcher of sweet tea I just made. I'll pour while you tell me all about Kayce and her extraordinary talent."

I smiled. "Look who's being snarky."

Daisy smiled sweetly. "Oh, no, I'm sure she's every bit as talented as Carter."

We had gotten back to the house a little after six o'clock, but I was so exhausted that I took a nap. I knew I would regret it when bedtime rolled around later, but I didn't care. When I woke up, I found Daisy sitting on the couch, a pile of baby clothes around her.

"My mom saved all of my old clothes. Can you believe it?" Daisy held up a neon pink onesie. "Hello, nineteen-eighties."

"Oh, good, your baby can rock the retro look," I said, laughing. I found a patch of empty couch and patted Daisy on the leg. "How are you doing, anyway? We've been so wrapped up in my problems that I have totally neglected you."

"I'm fine. Just be glad I got past my morning sickness phase before you and Maxwell moved in. Otherwise, you'd be on your own for breakfast each morning."

Daisy's spirit was indomitable. Nothing had diminished her joy or her optimism. I felt a sudden wave of guilt as I watched her happily sorting through clothes. "I'm so sorry, Daze," I said abruptly. "It's not fair for us to put you and Shaun through all of this. Maxwell and I need to find somewhere else to go. Now that there are demons on our trail, too, it's not safe for us to stay here."

Daisy shook her head firmly. "I already said that I think you're safest here."

"From the demon hunters, maybe. But demons aren't going to hesitate to hurt you just because you're pregnant."

Daisy sighed, put down a tiny flowered dress, and took my hands in her own. "You're my best friend, Betty. I understand the risk that Shaun and I are taking, and you aren't going to talk me out of it. I will do whatever I can to help you. So will Shaun."

"But—"

"It's not up for discussion. Don't say another word about it."

There was just no arguing with Daisy. "Thank you."

"You're welcome. Oh, and by the way, you need to go put your Seekers shirt back on."

"Why?"

"Because your work isn't done yet." Daisy's smile widened. "You said you wanted to get out of the house, so I've made plans for you."

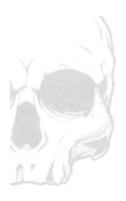

TWELVE

I had simply wanted to go out for dinner. Daisy had come up with a far more ambitious plan. While I had been napping, she had been on the phone to Carlo. The Seekers —plus Carter and his entourage—would all be going to Carlo's to try to win over his ghosts.

My efforts to convince Daisy that it was unnecessary were futile. As a demon, Carlo could easily communicate with his spectral residents. He could assure them that there was no reason to be angry with me, if he wished. Since he was on rather friendly terms with them, I was sure their violence wasn't directed at him. But no matter how many points I brought up, Daisy insisted on sticking to her plan.

"He saved your life last night," Daisy assured me.

"And I thanked him for it, believe me. I have no desire to see Carlo again, and I doubt that he has any desire to see me."

"Well, you don't have to see him for long. He's going to give us the run of his house again." Daisy hesitated. "In fact, I think he wants to be absent while we try to communicate with the ghosts."

"Told you so. And what do you mean, 'We'?"

"I'm going. Carlo promised it wouldn't be dangerous, and I want to see Carter's psychic friend in action."

We got to Carlo's house around ten o'clock. I shifted

nervously as we waited for him to answer the front door. It felt awkward seeing him again after he had admitted that he'd wanted to cash me in for the reward being offered. Of course, it would be a lot more awkward if he hadn't changed his mind. At least now I knew that he wasn't going to try to kill me.

Hopefully he hadn't changed his mind yet again.

Carlo was immaculately dressed, and I wondered if he owned anything other than suits. His eyes found mine as he greeted us, and he gave me a quick wink. "You are well?" he said lightly as he waved us inside.

"I'm sore all over, but I'm alive."

Carlo introduced himself to Maxwell. They shook hands cordially, but I could feel the tension between them. I guess demons can be a little territorial.

As we walked down the hallway, Carlo leaned in and spoke in a low voice. "I am in trouble with the demons. They aren't happy that I took you away from them."

"Do they know you didn't kill me?"

"If they do, they haven't let on. They will find out eventually, when they realize that the reward is still being offered."

"Maybe I'll have at least a few days of quiet."

Carter and the others had already arrived. We had a huge group there for what would be a quick process for just Kayce and me. Carlo excused himself, telling us to simply lock the door on our way out. He did seem anxious to leave. If the other demons were angry with him, then he probably didn't want to increase their ire by hanging out with me. Before he left, though, he motioned to me to follow him to the front door. He hesitated before saying, "You know, Betty, I could talk to the boss about you."

"What would that accomplish?" I did not like the idea of Carlo and Satan discussing me over coffee...or whatever they drank in hell.

"Perhaps nothing. Sometimes, though, it is possible to work out a deal. Maybe we can get the other demons off your back."

I began ticking off points on my fingers. "First, why are you offering to do this? Second, what do you want in return? And third, asking for leniency on my behalf will probably only fan the flames. With my luck, the reward will be doubled just to spite me."

Carlo smiled appreciatively. "You have dealt with demons before, I see. Think about my offer. You don't have to answer now." Without waiting for a response, Carlo left, giving me another wink before he shut the door.

"Demons," I muttered under my breath as I returned to the living room.

Carter insisted on escorting Kayce upstairs to Carlo's bedroom. Daisy announced that she was coming, too, and both Mick and Dwayne were going to film. That left only Shaun and Maxwell, who figured they might as well come, too.

Kayce and I sat on the floor, nose to nose, just as we had at The Hex. I was still uncomfortable with Kayce's nearness, but at least I wasn't surprised by it this time. I closed my eyes and began to concentrate on the memory of Rob's attack, but Kayce squeezed my hands. "Hold on, I need to get the spirit in on this, too," she said.

A few moments later, Kayce said quietly, "Okay, we've got her. Now focus, Betty."

I brought the scene to life in my head once again, but as I did my vision began to waver. Shadows flitted in and out of the scene, as if I were at the movies and someone kept running in front of the projector. I was recalling the sound of the waves on the beach outside the room, but soon their rhythm was joined by another noise. It was soft at first, but as I held onto the memory, the sound increased. It was crying. Someone was crying in my memory, though it had never happened at the time. I had wanted to cry, certainly, but Rob wouldn't let me make a sound.

This time, I was the one who was shoved backward by some mental force. Maxwell was standing behind me, so I knocked into his legs. He held steady and gripped my shoulders. "Betty?" Maxwell's voice sounded far away.

I opened my eyes to find everyone in the room peering down at me, worry on their faces. "I'm okay," I said, but it sounded more like a question.

"That did not come from me," Kayce said.

"It sure felt like it. I feel like someone smacked my forehead with a baseball bat." I absently rubbed my forehead, expecting to find a knot there.

"The spirit did it. She'd had enough and broke the connection."

"Well, she didn't have to do it so violently."

"It affected her a lot more than the spirit at The Hex. She's a young girl, so your memory horrified her." Kayce sat back and turned her attention to one of the cameras behind me. "On a positive note, she understands that the demon hunters are not what they seemed."

"On to the ghost in the basement, then," Carter said. He was already moving toward the door when I stopped him.

"Wait," I said. "I want to try something. While I was focusing on my memory, I could hear the ghost crying. Even though Kayce was sending my vision to the ghost, the ghost's thoughts were seeping into my head. I want to try what we just did again, only I want Kayce to send the ghost's memories to me."

"Why?" Kayce was shifting uncomfortably.

"Because I want to know what she can tell me about Carlo."

"He's a demon. What else do you need to know?" Maxwell said.

126

"He's a demon who saved my life," I corrected. "I want to know if the ghost can give us any insight into that. Why does Carlo want to help me, when he could go after the reward his *boss*," I said the word with as much sarcasm as I could muster, "is offering for me?"

"It is odd," Maxwell admitted, "but I can't blame him for making an exception for you. I did."

"I just want to try. Can we, Kayce?"

Kayce still looked uncomfortable. This would be a new exercise for her, and I was sure she was worried about failing when there were cameras and an audience around her. After a moment, though, she agreed.

I took Kayce's hands again and tried to clear my own thoughts from my head. I didn't want any communication from the ghost to get lost in the clutter. I concentrated on my own breathing and the feeling of my chest rising and falling.

The memory that the ghost channeled through Kayce didn't arrive at once. Like her crying, the scene formed slowly. It started like a half-painted watercolor, and details began to fill in. We were in Carlo's bedroom, and he was standing at the window, gazing out.

"Maxwell? Of course I've heard of him," Carlo was saying into a cell phone. "She's not just dating a demon; she's dating one of the most successful demons to ever walk the earth."

Carlo paused, clearly listening to the voice at the other end, then laughed. "Her dating a demon does not surprise me—we can be charming when we want—but I'm surprised that he is dating her. I would have thought he had no interest in such distractions."

There was a longer pause, and Carlo said, "Yes, I can certainly understand that. Actually, I think I'd like to meet her. I want to see what kind of woman can make a demon fall in love. She must be extraordinary."

Carlo soon hung up, and the memory began to fade. Soon I was hearing and feeling my own breathing again, and I knew that the connection between the ghost and me had ended.

Kayce released my hands, but I kept my eyes closed as I tried to memorize what I'd just witnessed. I didn't like the idea of Maxwell being an extremely successful demon, but if this bounty on me involved him, then it was worth remembering. Had Satan put a target on my back because I was interfering with Maxwell's true purpose?

That would be a lot of trouble for both Maxwell and me.

When I did open my eyes, Carter was staring at me. "So what did you see? Do you know why Carlo saved your life?"

"I'm not really sure. He wanted to meet me just to see how Maxwell could have possibly fallen for me. He had told me that he saved me because I'm a good person. Maybe he meant it."

"Good people are usually the first ones demons go after." Carter crossed his arms over his chest, unsatisfied with my answer.

"Carter, you are more than welcome to chat with the ghost yourself. I'm about exhausted already, and we still have the bully in the basement to deal with." I was not looking forward to communicating with that ghost again. I still had scratch marks from where he'd gripped my hand during our first encounter.

Carter declined, and Maxwell eased me into a standing position. I hadn't recovered from the energy drain at The Hex, and communicating with the female ghost had quickly tired me. I walked downstairs slowly, especially on the stairs to the basement. My knees wobbled with each step.

When Kayce and I were in position on the concrete

floor of the basement, I motioned Maxwell down next to me. "If it looks like I'm getting hurt, break the connection and get me out of here," I said.

Maxwell just nodded grimly.

Kayce took my hands, and this time I knew to wait until she gave the okay. When she did, I brought up the same memory. I was really getting tired of reliving the experience over and over.

I held the memory still: the knife just plunged into my side, Rob's glasses half an inch down the bridge of his nose, my body crushed under his weight. I didn't know if the ghost was getting the message or not. I just held perfectly still, putting all of my concentration into presenting that single image.

And then Rob's arm twitched. I saw it in the peripheral vision of my mind. Before I could process what was happening, the knife slid out of my side and plunged in again. My body spasmed with the renewed pain. Rob's arm moved again, and the knife stabbed me with more vigor. Rob began to laugh, low and menacing, as he stabbed me repeatedly. I twisted my head so I could look down at my side, but all I could see was Rob's hand tight around the hilt, his fingers stained with my blood. "No," I whispered. If I shouted, Rob would kill me. He had told me to be quiet.

"Please." My voice was barely audible over Rob's laughing. His body began to rock back and forth in time with his stabbing motions, and there was a look of glee in his eyes.

"Maxwell, help me," I whispered.

There was a loud crack, and Rob disappeared. Instead I was looking up at wood beams. It took me several seconds to realize it was the ceiling of the basement. Maxwell was lying awkwardly underneath me, his arms wrapped around my body and our legs tangled together.

I rolled off Maxwell and sat up slowly. He would be okay, I knew. On the opposite side of the room, Carter and Kayce were in a similar stance. Kayce had a dazed look on her face, and she was crying softly.

Everyone in the room was staring at me.

I looked from one face to the other. "What?"

"Your body started to jerk like you were in the electric chair," Shaun said. He ran a hand nervously through his red hair, and I saw that he was shaking. "Maxwell tried to pull you away from Kayce, but it was like you two were bolted together."

"How did you separate us?" I was shaking, too.

"You asked me to help you," Maxwell said. "I put my hands over yours and Kayce's and did my best to remind the ghost that you've got a demon on your side."

"I think he got the message. He changed my memory, made it worse. Then everything just disappeared."

I put a hand against my side, expecting to feel blood there. I was relieved when my fingers came away dry. I sighed and slumped against Maxwell. "You okay, Kayce?" I called.

"Yes. I'm so sorry. He liked your memory. He thought you deserved it. I tried to break the connection, but he was holding on too tightly."

"I guess we didn't convince him," I said dryly.

"It wasn't a failure. He knows the truth now, at least."

"He just doesn't care," Carter added. "Ghosts usually retain the same personalities they had in life. This guy was the scum of the earth, apparently."

A glass jar full of nails and screws fell off a shelf and shattered next to Carter.

"Carlo did say that there is evil in this world besides demons," I said. "That's glaringly obvious now. Come on. Let's go before someone really gets hurt."

Maxwell pulled me to my feet, but my knees wouldn't

cooperate. No matter how hard I tried, I just couldn't stand by myself. I put my arm around Maxwell's shoulders and hobbled as far as the bottom of the staircase, but I couldn't make it any further. Maxwell scooped me up in his arms and carried me effortlessly. We stayed only long enough for Mick and Dwayne to do some interviews about the night's events, and then we left, locking Carlo's front door behind us.

"Good riddance," I said as we drove away. "I wonder if Carlo knows what a jerk he has in his basement."

"I'm sure he does," Daisy said, "though chances are the ghost treats Carlo with a lot more respect."

"Well, I'm going to call Carlo tomorrow and give him a full report, but something tells me he won't be very surprised."

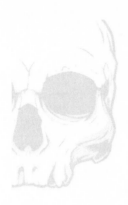

THIRTEEN

As I had suspected, Carlo was unsurprised to hear about his basement ghost's sadistic attitude. "I knew he had it in him," Carlo told me when I called him the next morning.

The only surprise during the conversation was on my end. Carlo expressed a great deal of regret over my treatment by the ghost, and he apologized several times. He even went so far as to wish he had stayed with us during the evening to keep his ghosts on better behavior.

I assured Carlo that no permanent damage had been done, but I was curious as to why he cared so much. His concern for my safety confused me. As much as Carlo claimed he had saved my life because I was a good person, I still felt like there was some other motive. Was Carlo just stringing me along, hoping to gain my trust and friendship before ultimately turning me in for the reward? It would be a very demonic thing to do: crush a person with betrayal before killing them.

Then again, Carlo wasn't making any effort to actually befriend me. The only reason I had seen him again was because of Daisy's insistence on talking to his ghosts.

It was just one more thing to add to my ever-growing "What the hell is going on?" list.

Instead of mulling over questions that I couldn't

possibly figure out an answer to, I called Grant Roberts and asked if The Seekers could come over to his house that night. I wasn't at all worried that his ghost would give me the kind of trouble Carlo's basement dweller had. Grant readily agreed, adding that, although his walls had remained graffiti free, he was still tripping over objects placed in his path.

After a quiet day of sitting around the house—thank goodness there was a classic movie marathon on TV—I was more than ready to head to Grant's house to wrap up the bizarre hauntings that we'd dealt with over the past week. I was grateful that the demon hunters hadn't recruited more ghosts, or we'd be chasing our tails endlessly in an effort to calm down all the agitated souls.

Grant was sitting on his front porch when we arrived that evening. It was far too cold to be relaxing outside, and I said as much to him. "I've been spending a lot of time out here," he admitted. "It just feels safer."

When I asked about the continued activity, Grant admitted that he'd only been having trouble with objects being moved to spots where he might trip over them. The knife throwing had come to an end. "Because," he explained sheepishly, "I've just stopped going into my kitchen altogether. I'm so afraid of having more knives thrown at me that I'm eating out for every meal."

Grant elected to stick around to see Kayce and me at work. It was a good thing he did: we were done in ten minutes. It took longer for Mick and Dwayne to set up and collect our body mics afterward than our actual work with the ghost. Grant was ecstatic, especially since Kayce relayed a message of apology from the ghost. "He says he won't cause this kind of trouble again, and he really wasn't trying to hit you with the kitchen knives. He just wanted to scare you."

Of course, we had to be vague when Grant asked why his ghost had been so angry in the first place, but we managed to explain it satisfactorily.

We were finished and back in our cars by nine o'clock. I felt better than I had in days, despite the energy drain. I was tired but happy. We had successfully dealt with all of the ghosts that the hunters had used to attack us (with the exception of Carlo's basement ghost, but some spirits are just lost causes).

Daisy turned around from the front seat. "Okay, Boo," she said, "since it was such a good night, I'm going to be nice and let you go out for dinner. Burglar Bar?"

"Gee, thanks, Mom," I said, laughing. "And yes, of course The Burglar Bar."

The Burglar Bar had been our hangout since college. It was a short walk from my apartment, but as we parked and walked to the entrance, the entire area felt strangely foreign. I had fled my apartment in fear of danger, and the usual warmth and contentment I normally felt in the historic district was missing tonight. It didn't feel like home anymore. I felt like a visitor, one whose map was upside down and backwards.

A burger, fries, and a glass of cabernet made me feel better. I smiled at the memory of meeting Maxwell there for the first time. He had approached me while I sat at a table up front, but tonight we sat in a booth at the very back of the restaurant, a framed mug shot of Al Capone watching over us as we ate. Maxwell and Shaun kept up a continual watch of the crowd, looking for anything suspicious, but we enjoyed a quiet celebration without interruption.

The streets felt a little more like home again when we emerged. It's amazing what a belly full of familiar food can do for the soul. I was tempted to pop into my apartment to grab some clothes, but Daisy forbade it. Maxwell and Shaun took her side, so I was out of luck.

For the ten-minute drive home, there was nothing wrong in my world. That feeling evaporated the moment we turned onto Shaun and Daisy's street and I saw Carter's Mercedes parked at the curb.

"Why is he here, and why didn't he call first?" Shaun said as we pulled into the driveway. Whatever his reason, we all knew it couldn't be good.

We didn't have to wonder for long. Carter, Kayce, Mick, and Dwayne all emerged from the car and hurried us inside the house. "It's not safe at my house anymore," Carter said as soon as we were inside. He watched Shaun lock the door, nodding with approval.

Once Carter assured us that all four of them were unharmed, we sat in the living room to hear his story.

"First, Daisy, can you grab a couple beers out of the fridge?" Carter began.

Daisy glared at him, and Carter nodded at Mick and Dwayne. "For them. They deserve it."

Daisy complied, looking a little less grumpy about it, though as she passed by me I heard her mutter, "Coulda said please."

Carter launched into his story as soon as Daisy had returned from the kitchen, saying, "I think the demon hunters have finally lost their patience. The ghosts didn't take care of us, and now they're getting frustrated and going on the attack."

Carter paused for dramatic effect, giving Mick's camera his most grim expression. Mick, I noticed, was deftly balancing his beer and the camera.

"Enough, Carter," I said.

"We grabbed a quick bite to eat after we left Grant's house," Carter continued. "When we pulled up in front of my house, nothing seemed out of the ordinary. Then I got to the front door. There are glass panels on either side of the door, and there's a mirror just inside the door. The reflection in the mirror was off somehow. Usually, at night, it just looks like a dull gray surface. Tonight, though, there were shadows in it."

"We thought he was just being paranoid," Dwayne said.

"It was like a hunch more than anything," Carter conceded. "But I suddenly felt like there was somebody— or something—waiting for me there on the other side of the door."

"Did you call the police?" Shaun asked.

"Is that why you came over here?" Daisy said simultaneously.

"Who was it?" I joined in.

Carter put his hands up like he was staving off a mob. "Calm down. No, I didn't call the police. All those demon hunters have to do is point authorities to all those dead bodies on Serenity Island, and we're in deep trouble. They haven't done so yet, so I think it's only wise that we stay away from the police, too."

He did have a point.

"I wanted to sneak around to the back so I could go in that way," Carter continued. "I thought if I took them by surprise that I might be able to get them out of the house. Dwayne and I went around, and Mick and Kayce stayed on the front porch. I wanted them there so it sill looked like we were coming in the front. Anyway, I unlocked the back door, and Dwayne and I charged into the house. I flicked on the hall light as we ran toward the front door, but there was no one there."

I felt strangely let down by the end of Carter's story. That was it? All that buildup, and it turned out that Carter really was just paranoid?

"We found him in my bedroom," Carter continued. Okay, now we were back on track. "He'd apparently fled up the stairs when he heard the back door. He was waiting with a gun in one hand and a knife in the other."

Now the story was a little *too* exciting for my taste. I pressed my hand to my mouth, visions of the hunters doing the same to Maxwell and me. Carter had stopped for another dramatic pause, and I waved urgently at him with my free hand.

"He made it onto my balcony and jumped down to the street before we could even cross the room," Carter said. "He landed on the sidewalk not ten feet from where Kayce and Mick were standing. He fired a shot at them over his shoulder."

Every pair of eyes turned to Mick and Kayce. Neither of them appeared to be bleeding, so presumably the hunter's shot had missed.

"Did you recognize him?" Maxwell's face was stern, his voice menacing.

Carter shook his head.

Daisy swore softly, got up, and disappeared into the kitchen. She reappeared a moment later and handed beers to Carter and Kayce. "I think you two need them, too," she said.

"It's strange that he was alone," Maxwell mused. "Hunters typically work alone, or with a partner, but that's when they're actually hunting demons. We know they have teamed up to come after us, so why was this guy alone? He should have had backup, or a lookout, or something. It's not congruous with the other incidents. Take my house, for example. They had their bases covered there."

"I also don't understand why he didn't shoot you," I said. "Sure, you caught him off guard, but he could have stood there and fired his gun at you before he jumped."

"It doesn't make sense," Carter said, "though I'm glad

that he didn't shoot me. Maybe we startled him so much that he was too afraid to attack."

"Or," I suggested, "he just wanted to scare you. He wanted you to feel unsafe in your own home."

"He wanted me to come here," Carter finished for me.

Everyone fell silent, thinking of the implications of that line of thinking. It was Maxwell who finally spoke, his voice ominously quiet. "They're not using a divide and conquer philosophy. They're trying to herd us into one place, like cattle."

I had never seen a pregnant lady move as fast as Daisy did at that moment. She was out of her chair and across the room in a blur, peering out the peephole on the front door. The grumblings coming from her weren't from fear, but from anger. When she turned to face all of us, her cheeks were flushed. "Maxwell, Betty, you take the back door. Shaun and I will guard the front. Carter and Kayce, you two will keep an eye on the nursery and guest bedroom. Mick and Dwayne, you've got guard duty in the master bedroom. I want everyone to take turns sleeping and keeping watch. We are going to turn off every light in this house, and I want eyes looking out at every moment. Understood?"

We all agreed, shocked by Daisy's take-charge attitude. Clearly, she had had enough of living in fear of an attack and was ready for some open warfare.

Within a few minutes we were all at our posts. Maxwell and I were in the kitchen. He was peering intently out the window next to the back door while I sat at the kitchen table, my leg bouncing up and down incessantly.

"I hate this," I said.

"I do, too, Betty." The back porch light silhouetted Maxwell's body, and I could tell he had turned his body toward me. "I'm ready to have this over with, though. If it means we fight the hunters tonight, then so be it."

"This isn't Daisy and Shaun's fight. I don't want them in danger."

"Neither do I. That gives us only one other option: we flee. Now. If that's what you want to do, then we'll do it."

I bit my lip. If Maxwell wasn't promoting the idea, then he had some reason to think it wasn't a good one. "But?" I prompted.

"You have friends who care about you. There's safety in numbers." I knew Maxwell was trying to be reassuring, but it sounded cruel.

"What, I'm supposed to sacrifice my friends for my own safety?"

"Also, we're indoors, and there are only so many points from which the hunters could gain access." Maxwell completely ignored my question. He didn't want our friends to get hurt—or worse—any more than I did, but he was going to do everything in his power to give us a better chance at victory.

I laughed mirthlessly. "What a turn my life has taken. I'm barricaded in my best friend's house because a pack of demon hunters is after me. If we survive this, Carter's next book is going to be a best-seller."

"Oh, do you think he'll write a book about all this?" Kayce's voice spoke up from the doorway. I could barely make out her form in the ambient light.

"Probably. It is Carter, after all," I said. "Everything okay?"

"Yeah, I just wanted a soda." There was a blinding flare of light as Kayce opened the fridge, and a moment later I heard the crack of a can being opened.

I told Kayce to stay with Maxwell so I could go check on Carter. The hallway was much darker than the kitchen, and I groped my way to the nursery. Carter was outlined in the window, but his shoulders slumped in a way I'd never seen before. Carter Lansford was not a man who was easily defeated, but judging by his body language, he was on the verge of surrender.

Impulsively, I moved next to Carter and wrapped my arms around him. He stiffened at first, but after a moment he relaxed and rested his chin on top of my head. "I'm so sorry, Carter," I whispered.

Carter's voice was strained when he answered. "I am, too. I never should have taken you to Serenity Island."

"You can't be blaming this on yourself."

I felt Carter's head nod.

"Don't be ridiculous. Maxwell is blaming himself, too. I'm the one who stuck a knife in a hunter. If you want to get technical, it's my fault. Personally, though, I'm blaming the hunters for this. They're the ones who set us up at Serenity Island. We had to fight back."

Carter just nodded again, more resolutely this time, though.

"We need to talk about our options," I said carefully. "Do we stay here or do we run?"

"I can't answer that. If we stay, everyone else is at risk. If we run, they might still be at risk. Mick and Kayce got shot at, so I don't think the hunters' revenge is reserved for just the three of us. It might be safer for them if we *don't* run."

"But if we run, we'll draw their attention away from our friends," I argued.

"I don't have the answer. I've never felt this helpless in my entire life." Carter's voice cracked, and I silently begged him not to cry. I didn't think I could stand to see the proudest, most confident man I'd ever met break down. If he lost hope, then how could I hang onto it myself?

Poor Carter. He'd been given everything his whole life: his house, his money, and, I suspected, his friends, who were drawn to his wealth and social standing. Now, other than the souls inside the house with him, he had no help in trying to save his own life. There was no check he could write to stave off the hunters.

My arms were still around Carter, and I gave him a squeeze. "Are you and Kayce dating?" I suddenly asked. I wanted a change of subject before Carter got too melancholy, and it was the first thing that popped into my head.

Carter made a derisive sound. "No. The latest incident is still a little too fresh in my mind." Carter had gotten involved with the housekeeper on Serenity Island. She had drugged him, since she was the daughter of a demon hunter and as bent on catching Maxwell as the other hunters.

Yes, Carter was definitely right in being more cautious in his dating choices.

"I had a thought, Betty," Carter said, his voice low. "I don't think Lou is the one who had the ghosts attack us. It's not like him."

"Then who did? No one else knows so much about our investigations."

Carter hesitated. "The hunters already knew about the revenants. The other cases are detailed on my website."

"Oh." I was tempted to make a snarky comment about Carter's need for publicity, but he was already feeling low. Plus, it made me feel a lot better to think that Lou might not have been behind the attacks.

We fell silent, but we stayed there together at the window until I heard Kayce bumping her way into the room. "Am I interrupting something?" she asked, the insinuation clear.

"Not at all," I said. "Carter was just consoling me since a bunch of well-armed men want us dead."

As I passed by Kayce, I could feel her eyes on me. I was barely in the hall before she asked Carter archly, "And what was that all about?"

I could have turned around and told Kayce that she

had no reason to be jealous. There was no chance that I would ever fall for Carter. Instead, I decided to let her stew. It just wasn't worth getting into. I did have to smile at Carter's claim that he and Kayce weren't dating. Clearly, Kayce felt otherwise.

Maxwell tried to talk me into napping so I would be refreshed when it was my turn to keep watch. I dutifully put my head down on the table, but my brain wouldn't shut off. The house was silent despite there being eight of us in it, and the lack of noise or movement was disconcerting. It felt unnatural.

Shaun passed through the house a short while later, when I'd given up on sleeping and reverted to bouncing my leg nervously. "It's one a.m.," Shaun announced. "Things looking good here?"

Maxwell assured him that all was well, and Shaun passed on to the next room.

I was on watch when Shaun came through again, telling us that it was three in the morning. Kayce had had the right idea of raiding the fridge for caffeine earlier, and a big glass of sweet tea was my companion while I stared out the window. Unfortunately, that meant that I was also keeping a dutiful watch over the bathroom. Maxwell wasn't sleeping, but we didn't converse much. We had little to say on the subject of the hunters, and it felt weird trying to make light conversation.

When the silence of the house really started to get to me, I turned to Maxwell. "You once promised to tell me about the war," I said.

Maxwell laughed softly. "Which one?" He knew the answer already, and after a brief pause, he began. "I was in Milledgeville when Georgia seceded from the Union. Did you know that Milledgeville was the state capital then? They didn't move the seat of government to Atlanta until after the war.

"I dealt in cotton back then. Farmers brought their cotton crops to me, and I sold it for them. I was a middle man, if you will."

"A factor," I supplied. The lane behind the long line of old cotton warehouses down by the Savannah River was still called Factor's Walk. Those buildings housed shops and restaurants now, but their history wasn't forgotten.

"That's right. Cotton was king, so that made me a sort of prince, I guess. I got to live in the city, making good money off cotton, without ever having to step foot in a field. Things were perfect until we seceded. A lot of boys rushed off to fight for the Confederacy, but business continued as usual, even once the war broke out.

"As it went on, though, things began to fall apart. Blockades along the coast meant I couldn't export cotton to interested buyers abroad, and that was if there was even cotton to be sold. A lot of it was going to make uniforms and blankets for soldiers. Anything and everything went toward war supplies, and extra money went into war bonds. Even I bought some, though I started to quietly tuck away my money. I'd been through enough wars to know the risks."

"Did you fight?" I asked. I definitely didn't see Maxwell as a soldier, fighting for someone else's cause.

"In my own way. When Sherman and his men came through Georgia late in the war, they burned everything in their path, including what precious crops we had left. I knew the end was coming soon. The South just had nothing left to fight with. It didn't stop me from having a little fun at the Yankees' expense, though. They spared Milledgeville, taking up residence in our government build-ings and our nice houses. My home was no exception: a general and his men moved right in. A lot of folks had fled, but I stayed behind and, well, did my demonic best with the general. By the time the Union army left Milledgeville, the general had gone mad. A few of his men were on the brink, and one of them committed suicide. He hanged himself from the oak tree in my front yard."

I shuddered. Maxwell's voice held a note of pride, and I was reminded of the wide divide between his life and mine. It was easy to forget that he was a demon, but things like this made the truth far too clear.

"They left Milledgeville and came to Savannah," I said, hoping that moving the story along would get the image of a dead soldier swinging from a noose out of my head.

"That's right. General Sherman presented this city to President Lincoln as a damn Christmas present." Maxwell paused, absorbed in his memories. "After the war ended, things were slow to pick up. I headed to Savannah in the hope of finding a new career. I had a lot more money than the people who threw it all away on war bonds, so it was easy to get into business. I'd made Savannah my home before, and it felt natural to do it again."

"What was it like during the war? Were you scared?"

"No. What did I have to be scared of? At first I found some joy in it. Seeing all those women crying over the coffins that came in on the trains. Boxcar after boxcar of dead soldiers. War is a great tool for demons. It practically does our work for us. Then my friends and business associates began coming home, either in coffins or missing limbs. That made me sad, actually. I was fine with the world at large falling apart, but not my world."

"If you knew the South was going to lose, why didn't you head north?" Surely Maxwell hadn't been patriotic about the Confederacy.

"I guess I'm stubborn. But amid the loss, there was also great opportunity. Or, at least, I knew there would be. I just had to wait things out, like we're doing right now."

Maxwell's voice sounded distant as I stared out the window. My skin turned to ice. "I think the wait is over," I said.

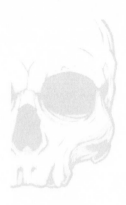

FOURTEEN

Maxwell was immediately by my side. A low growl emanated from the back of his throat when he saw the hunter edging toward the house. "Stay perfectly still," Maxwell breathed into my ear. With that, he disappeared.

I knew Maxwell was telling everyone else, materializing in each room to report, but I felt like I was the only person left in the house. The hunter was creeping through the backyard, inch by inch, just a shadow in the darkness. Every step he took terrified me. He was moving in slow motion, and it only drew out my anxiety.

By the time Maxwell returned, the hunter was just coming into the pool of yellow cast by the porch light. As the hunter's massive bulk and stern face came into view, I gasped. Maxwell stiffened next to me.

"That's him," I said. It was pointless to articulate the thought further; Maxwell and I both recognized the hunter who had come after him at Fort Pulaski. That night, I had thought the hunter was successful.

So had the hunter.

Clearly, he had now realized his error. It felt all wrong that this man was coming after us. I had run into the hunter at the cathedral one afternoon, and he had been almost kind to me. I couldn't believe that he was now part of the group that wanted me dead.

Everyone is against us, I thought wildly. We're never getting out.

The hunter was only fifteen feet away from the back door, and I didn't even know what the plan was. Maxwell must have sensed my confusion, because he whispered calmly, "We let him in."

"We can't let him in!"

"If we go outside, they might have the advantage in numbers. If we let them in one at a time, we have the advantage." By "advantage," I assumed Maxwell meant "opportunity to kill." I did not like the idea of slaughtering demon hunters in Daisy and Shaun's kitchen.

The hunter had crept onto the back porch. He carefully pulled a silver knife out of a sheath on his belt.

I silently sprinted to the other side of the kitchen and pulled a knife from the butcher's block on the counter. I couldn't see what size knife I drew, but it felt heavy and strangely reassuring. I'd already killed one man with a knife. If it came down to it, I could do it again.

But I still really, really didn't want to.

The moral battle raging in my head came to an abrupt stop as the handle on the back door creaked. Did the hunter really think that we would just leave the door unlocked?

"I'll get it," I whispered. I didn't want Maxwell anywhere near that silver knife. I stepped forward, took a deep breath, and unlocked the door. Before I could second-guess myself, I swung the door wide. "Well, hey!" I said loudly. I hoped it would catch him off guard.

It did. The hunter stepped back in surprise. Maxwell dove in low and grabbed the hunter around the knees. With one hefty yank, the hunter fell backwards. Maxwell pulled him inside the kitchen, and I shut the door.

The hunter was already clambering to his feet, and Maxwell somehow pushed him down again. It was too dark to see what was going on. I expected the others to come to our aid, but no one did. Instead, I heard a shout that sounded like it came from Shaun and a high-pitched scream. I was pretty sure it was Kayce, but I didn't rule out Carter, either.

I heard another shout, but this time it was Maxwell. I fumbled for the light switch, and when my eyes adjusted to the sudden brightness, I saw a horrible tableau before me. The hunter had pulled Maxwell down on top of him. As they fought, the silver knife flashed again and again. It cut Maxwell but had yet to make the fatal blow to his heart.

The only thought that my brain could process was "get the knife away from the hunter." I dropped my own knife, fell to my knees beside the two men, and grabbed the hunter's arm. I couldn't compete with his strength, so I put my mouth on his forearm and bit down as hard as I could.

The hunter bellowed but didn't stop fighting Maxwell. We were all in a pile next to the table, and I snatched a seat cushion off one of the wooden chairs. I shoved it as hard as I could against the hunter's face, hoping that the lack of sight and oxygen would slow him down. It seemed to take ages before his movements lessened, but finally Maxwell was able to get the upper hand as the hunter's struggles weakened.

When the hunter's arms went limp and fell to his sides, Maxwell grabbed the silver knife. "No!" I shouted.

Maxwell actually laughed as he tossed the knife away from him. "Why would I stab him? That's so messy."

"No incinerating, either," I said. "Please. I don't want either one of us killing someone in this house."

Maxwell looked disappointed, but he agreed. "Keep the pillow over his face. Don't worry, it won't kill him." Maxwell rummaged in the kitchen drawers until he triumphantly pulled out a roll of plastic wrap. "Let's turn him over," Maxwell instructed.

When the hunter was on his stomach, Maxwell quickly bound the man's hands behind him with a long length of plastic wrap. "You're kidding, right? How is that going to hold him?" I knew we didn't have the luxury of rope or actual handcuffs, but plastic wrap?

Maxwell smiled. "Trust me. If you wrap this stuff thick and tight enough, it's impossible to get out of without a knife."

I didn't ask Maxwell how he knew that.

We had only a split second to enjoy our victory before we heard the sound of glass breaking. It seemed to come from every direction at once. Kayce screamed again, and then amid the din, I heard Daisy shouting a lecture that sounded vaguely like the "Does your mother know what you're doing?" variety. I scooped up the hunter's knife, and we followed the sound to find one of the oddest sights I'd ever seen.

A hunter was crawling through a living room window while Daisy lectured him and Shaun beat him over the head with his grandmother's cuckoo clock. They seemed to have the hunter covered, so Maxwell and I continued down the hall to the bedrooms.

Mick and Dwayne were also fighting off a hunter, a skinny guy who had wriggled through a broken window in the master bedroom. Dwayne was actually filming while Mick wrestled the hunter to the ground. The hunter squirmed but didn't have the muscles that Mick did. "Dwayne, grab the plastic wrap from the kitchen!" I shouted as we passed their doorway. "Tie him up!"

We reached the nursery in time to see Carter fall backwards, a hunter crashing down on top of him. Kayce shoved past Maxwell and me, screaming and running in a blind hysteria.

Kayce got four feet down the hallway when a masculine arm shot out of the guest bedroom doorway. Our bedroom, I thought suddenly. Kayce slapped at the arm, but the hunter's fingers curled around her upper arm and clamped tight.

"I got you!" the hunter shouted. "Hah, I won!"

I started to run to Kayce's aid, but Maxwell stopped me with an arm around my waist. "He thinks that she's you. I'll help Kayce. You help Carter."

The hunter emerged from the bedroom and began dragging Kayce behind him, heading for the front door. Maxwell stalked up behind him, but before he attacked, I turned my attention to Carter. The nursery had gotten crowded when I wasn't looking. Two more hunters had crawled through the window. Carter was not only pinned to the ground, but he was surrounded. To his credit, he continued to fight, even though it was futile.

I shouted for help, which only drew the attention of the hunters. Two of them stayed with Carter, but the third walked slowly toward me. His wide mouth grinned triumphantly, a ghastly sight in his pockmarked and leathery face.

Every hunter looks so rough, I thought. Don't these guys ever pamper themselves?

No, I realized. Being a demon hunter was a hard life. Lou was going to look like this someday: downtrodden and haggard. Like he was fighting a battle he could never actually win.

Mr. Smiley certainly wasn't going to win tonight. I planted my feet in the doorway and let him come to me. I kept my knife hidden, my arms at my sides and the blade just behind my thigh. I made my best scared-to-death face so he might let his guard down.

"I've never banished a demon, but at least I'll be able to say I killed a demon's whore," Mr. Smiley said. His eyes locked on mine, but in the corner of my eye, I saw the gun in his hand. Either it was loaded with silver bullets, or he had come simply to kill humans.

"Enjoy hell," he snarled. His arm came up, and the gun was against my forehead before I could react. I froze. In my panic, my only thought was that I didn't want to shed blood in the baby's room. I thought about pleading my case, but I knew that wouldn't work. I was out of options.

Mr. Smiley's head suddenly cocked at an odd angle, and his neck made a crunching sound. He fell to the floor, dead, and I looked up to find myself face-to-face with Maxwell. He had materialized behind the hunter.

Before I could so much as say thanks, Maxwell pivoted and turned his attention to the other two hunters. The one who wasn't tangled up with Carter drew his knife just as Maxwell disappeared. The hunter stood, slack-jawed, for only seconds before Maxwell materialized behind him and snapped his neck, as well.

If the hunter hadn't been smart enough to expect that after seeing Maxwell do it to Mr. Smiley, then I couldn't really feel sorry for him. I did, however, feel sorry about the fact that there were now two dead bodies in the nursery. So much for my request that we not kill anyone.

The third hunter proved to be smarter than his companion. The second body hadn't even settled onto the floor when he released Carter and hurled himself out the window. I didn't think we would need to worry about him coming back.

Carter was relatively unhurt—I knew he'd lament the tears in his designer clothes later—so we moved swiftly down the hallway. The guest bedroom was clear. The skinny hunter that Mick had tackled lay bound on the floor of the master bedroom. Maxwell's handiwork in the kitchen remained untouched, and there were two unconscious (or dead; I wasn't sure which) hunters on the living room floor. Kayce was crouched in a corner of the room, sobbing hysterically. Shaun was bruised and disheveled, and Daisy was actually smiling.

"I think we won," she said.

"What do we do with them all?" Carter was looking at the hunters with distaste. "We can't just hold them hostage."

"We could," Maxwell suggested.

"No," I spoke up. "We let them go. Show them more kindness than they've shown to us."

"Are you insane? After what they've done to us, they deserve at least a little suffering!" Carter looked like he was mentally making a list of said suffering.

"They do deserve it," I agreed, "but we're better people than they are. If you ask them why they're doing this to us, they'll just say it's because we deserve it."

Daisy sniffed, and for a moment I thought she was going to start crying, too. I was about to tell her not to be a Kayce when she said, "Do you smell something burning?"

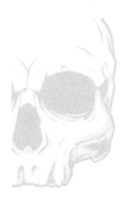

FIFTEEN

We all sniffed simultaneously. Daisy's sense of smell must have been heightened by her pregnancy because I didn't smell anything. Maxwell did, though, and without a word, he ran into the kitchen.

All of us had our eyes trained on the doorway to the kitchen, expecting Maxwell to return through it, when he materialized right in front of Daisy. She let out a startled yelp as Maxwell's hands clamped down on her shoulders. "You have to leave, now," he said. "Shaun, get Daisy as far away from this house as you can."

Daisy was still begging for an explanation as Shaun took her by the hand and pulled her to the front door. When he opened it, a wave of smoke blew in. The front yard was on fire, but the flames hadn't yet reached the front door. There was still a clear path to the driveway. Shaun and Daisy ran for it. They reached Shaun's car, and I waited breathlessly while they clambered inside. I expected them to be attacked at any moment, but they got in and were gone before I realized that they were safe.

Maxwell slammed the front door shut. "They're probably out there waiting for us. They've set the back yard on fire, too, and they're going to wait for us to come out so they can pick us off."

"But Daisy and Shaun...," I began.

"Got away because Daisy was right: they won't hurt a pregnant woman," Maxwell finished.

"How can there be any of them left? Other than the one who ran off, they're all either dead or tied up," Carter said.

"Clearly there were more." Maxwell's face was grim.

Another wave of smoke drifted into the room, this time from the kitchen. The fire had burned through the back yard and reached the house. "What about the windows in the bedrooms? We might get out that way," Carter said.

Maxwell and Carter shared a look of hope before they took off down the hall to check. When they came back, Carter was coughing. "That whole end of the house is on fire already," Maxwell said.

That left us with two options: stay inside the house and be burned alive, or make a run for it and get shot or stabbed before we could even reach the street. I turned to Mick and Dwayne, who were taking this latest turn of events with surprising calm. "I am so sorry," I said.

"I liked the violent ghosts a whole lot better than these demon hunters," Mick said. His voice was so flat that I figured he was either in shock or just incredibly brave.

"Does somebody have a plan?" Unlike Mick's, my voice had a twinge of panic.

No one answered. As we stood there, silently contemplating which doom we would choose, Kayce finally got up from her spot in the corner. She walked right past us into the kitchen. She reappeared in the doorway a moment later, a cold soda in her hand. "We take hostages," she said calmly. Definitely in shock, I thought.

"There are four hunters in here," Carter said, "and five of us, if Maxwell can just beam himself elsewhere. We could take them out with us."

I shook my head. "I don't think they care about saving

each other. Someone set this place on fire knowing full well there were hunters in here."

"Sacrificing someone you can't see or hear is one thing," Carter said. "Sacrificing someone who's standing right in front of you is another. But if we're going to get them, we need to move fast."

Carter was right. The smoke was getting thicker, and I heard one of the kitchen windows shatter as the heat and pressure became too much. Dwayne and Carter headed down the hall to get the skinny hunter from the master bedroom, while Maxwell and Mick raced into the kitchen to get the other hunter. As we waited for them to return, I spotted something long, thin, and black sticking out from underneath the couch.

Mina.

Things had been so crazy that I had entirely forgotten about my cat. My purse was sitting on the couch where I'd thrown it when we had come in earlier in the night. I grabbed it, pulled Mina out of her hiding spot, and shoved her in my purse. Daisy always made fun of me for having a big purse, but now it was just what I needed. I slung it over my shoulder and hoped Mina would forgive me for the rough treatment.

Both of the hunters from the other rooms were now awake, which was good, since the one who had tried to kill Maxwell at Fort Pulaski was too big to be carried. That left us with the two unconscious guys on the living room floor. I didn't know what Shaun had done to them, but he had done a good job of it.

Mick hoisted one of the unconscious hunters over his shoulder, and Carter volunteered to take the lighter of the two. That left the burly hunter in Dwayne's care, and Kayce and I each grabbed one of Skinny's arms.

"What now? Do we wave a white flag, run out there using these guys as shields, or what?" I looked from one face to another, hoping to find someone with a definitive plan.

"First of all, I'll do my best to distract them," Maxwell said. "Second, I think you were right when you said that about us being better people than them, Betty. I'm not technically 'people,' but we won't argue semantics right now. We need to take them out there like we're saving their lives. It might give the hunters pause, and maybe we can get away before they think better of returning our kindness."

Maxwell handed me his car keys. "Take mine. I'll meet you at the corner of Victory and Abercorn. And good luck." Maxwell leaned in and kissed me, which was slightly awkward considering I was hanging onto a demon hunter. Still, if our plan failed, it would be the last kiss I ever shared with Maxwell—or with anyone, for that matter—so I tried to savor it.

With a pop, Maxwell disappeared. Then I heard another pop, and another. Were demons materializing inside the house? I looked around and saw flames licking their way up the hallway. No, it wasn't demons making that sound. It was the house, burning down around us.

"Leave your hunter next to your car and get out of here as fast as you can," Carter shouted. "Go!" He was the first out the door, his arms tight around the back of his hunter's legs. Mick and Dwayne followed closely behind him, and Kayce and I emerged last.

The flames had spread, and the gravel walk that led to the driveway had become a narrow corridor surrounded by fire. Thankfully, Skinny realized how dire our situation was, and he hustled so quickly that Kayce lost her grip on him.

All I could see was fire on both sides and the bobbing head of the hunter slung over Mick's shoulder in front of me. I didn't know what awaited us once we reached the driveway.

When my feet hit the concrete of the driveway, I didn't see Carter lying there dead. That was a good sign, at least. I stayed in line with the others until we reached the curb. Carter darted left to get to his car, and Mick, Dwayne, and Kayce followed. That left just Skinny and me, bearing right to Maxwell's car.

I felt exposed once I was away from the others. Carter shouted something back at me, but I couldn't hear him over the noise of the fire and my own gasping breaths. I realized there was another sound, too, growing steadily as I narrowed the distance to the car. Sirens.

There were dead people inside the house, and I did not want to be on the scene when the firefighters showed up.

Apparently, Skinny didn't want to be questioned by the authorities, either. He wrenched his arm out of my grip and went sprinting down the street. Good riddance, I thought. I had reached Maxwell's car, and I made it safely inside. I started the car, put it in first gear, and gave one parting glance to Daisy and Shaun's house.

The roof was on fire now, too. I forced myself to look at the street, and I tore away, hoping none of the neighbors would report the Audi R8 that was so blatantly fleeing the scene.

I turned the corner and passed the fire truck. They wouldn't be able to save the house, but maybe they could keep the fire from spreading through the neighborhood.

I pulled up at the corner of Victory and Abercorn a few minutes later. Maxwell, as promised, was already there, casually leaning against a street sign. He came to the driver's side, so I hopped out to let him take over. "Everyone away safely?" he asked.

"I think so. I was the last one out of there."

Maxwell caught me in a brief hug before jumping in

the car. He didn't have to tell me that he was worried I had been followed. I hurried to the passenger side, and Maxwell took off at a speed that made me think his driving might be more terrifying than the hunters.

"Where are we going?" I would wear permanent nail marks in the dash if Maxwell didn't slow down.

"To the place that I made home the last time I had to flee Savannah."

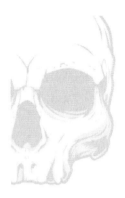

SIXTEEN

Maxwell's speed only increased once we reached the interstate. We went west and picked up Interstate 95, going north. We drove in silence for the first half hour, Maxwell too focused on driving and me too worried we might die in a horrific crash. I let Mina out of my purse and she was also quiet, sitting demurely on my lap.

I jumped when a high-pitched beeping began. I had forgotten that my cell phone was in my back pocket.

It was Daisy. "Please tell me you're alive," she said. Her voice was thick, and I knew she had been crying.

"I'm still here. We all made it out safely."

"My house, Betty."

My eyes filled with tears at the despair in Daisy's voice. I wiped absently at them with my hand and wrinkled my nose. I reeked of smoke. "Daisy, I'm sorry." I had been saying that too much tonight. "This is our fault. Maxwell and I should have never come to your house."

"I was the one who insisted. You can't blame yourself. Where are you two going to go, anyway?"

"I don't know. We're heading north. What about you?"

"We're going to Macon to stay with my parents. Keep me posted, okay?"

I agreed and hung up the phone, feeling absolutely dejected. The pain in Daisy's voice broke my heart. She and Shaun had lost their home and all their belongings. The nursery that they had been working so hard to make comfortable for their baby had been destroyed. What was even worse was the feeling that I would never be able to make this up to Daisy. I had already lost Lou, and I couldn't handle losing my best friend, too.

To stave off the crying fit that I felt building up inside, I called Carter. They, too, had gotten away safely. Carter didn't know where they were going, just that it was south.

We were scattered. After being manipulated into coming together under the same roof, we were now moving farther apart from each other with every mile.

I breathed deeply and focused on petting Mina, still trying to hold off the tears. I glanced over at Maxwell, who was rubbing his thumb and forefinger together, creating sparks. His gaze was intent on the road ahead, and I wasn't sure he even remembered that I was with him. Maxwell finally felt my eyes on him and turned to me. He slowed down, though we were still well above the speed limit, and took my hand, drawing it over to rest on his leg.

Maxwell's touch made me feel better, but eventually I couldn't hold back my tears. I just needed a good cry. We'd been attacked, Maxwell had killed two men with his bare hands, and my best friend's house had been burned. I also didn't know if it would ever be safe to return to Savannah, and I wondered how long it would be before the hunters who weren't dead regrouped and came looking for us. I knew it was only a matter of time. All we had done tonight was fuel their hatred.

Amid all of those thoughts, I also considered Lou. He had claimed that the hunters wouldn't hurt us, but they had obviously changed their mind on that. Had Lou changed his mind, too? Or were they acting behind Lou's back?

Demon hunters usually collected their bounties from

priests. I seriously doubted that the church would approve of what the hunters had done tonight. They were operating under their own moral code now.

My crying slowed when Maxwell dove off at an exit. My curiosity outweighed my sorrow, and I asked again, "Where are we going?"

"The back way."

Maxwell stopped for gas, and while he pumped, looking suspiciously at every car that pulled into the station, I ran inside and got some drinks and snacks. I didn't know how far we were going, but I was hungry and my throat was parched from inhaling smoke.

Soon we were underway again, driving down a two-lane road that stretched past farms and acres of woods. There were no more city lights, and I felt isolated. When I said so to Maxwell, he just nodded. "That's the point. On the interstate, there are too many cars to tell if one of them is following us. Out here, we'll know if we have a tail."

I craned my head around and looked out the back window, afraid I'd see headlights suddenly appear right behind our bumper, like some kind of horror movie. Thankfully, there was only blackness stretching out behind us.

"You should get some sleep," Maxwell said.

"I don't think I'll be able to." I yawned before the words were out of my mouth. I was mentally and physically exhausted. I closed my eyes and laid my head back against the headrest.

"Sweet dreams, Betty," Maxwell said.

I reached over and squeezed his arm. "Whatever happens, Maxwell, I'm glad that I have you with me."

It was still dark when I woke up. I opened my eyes just in time to see the sign for the street we were turning onto: Maxwell Farm Road.

"You have a farm?" I asked, still groggy.

"I used to. I've sold off the farmland, but I still have a few acres where the house is."

In a mile, we turned onto a narrow dirt road. It wound back through a wooded area and finally emerged in an overgrown clearing. A pretty two-story house sat in the middle. It had a wide front porch and gabled windows across the second story. Even with the headlights as our only illumination, I could tell that the house was run down. The white paint was dull, and one shutter was missing from a window.

"I have people who maintain it, but it really needs a thorough restoration," Maxwell said apologetically. "Still, it's been retrofitted with plumbing and electricity, so we should be all right. We'll go to the store tomorrow and get things."

"Will we be safe here?"

"I don't think we're safe anywhere. However, I don't think we were followed."

Maxwell pulled around the back. He didn't have the key to the house, but he materialized inside and opened the back door for me.

We were in the kitchen, and when Maxwell turned on the lights, I saw horribly outdated appliances. The façade of the house was historic, but the interior was retro. The Formica countertops, squat fridge, and yellow oven all screamed 1950s. Still, everything was neat and clean, which was enough for me.

Maxwell locked up the back and led me toward the stairs. "I haven't been here in a few years. Since I don't age, I try not to put in too many appearances. In a small place like this, people notice, and they talk."

"What town is this, anyway?"

"Dewy Rose. The closest big city is Athens."

"How did you ever wind up in a place like this?"

We were halfway up the broad staircase before Maxwell answered, "I said I had to flee Savannah once before. I had been living there happily after the war when a new priest was installed at the cathedral. He was from Europe, and he took demonology and the supernatural a lot more seriously than his predecessor. I don't know how, but he knew what I was from the start. It was like he just had the sight."

"So you packed up and moved to the middle of nowhere?" Maxwell was not a country boy, by any means. A secluded house surrounded by farmland just didn't seem like his thing.

"One of the cotton planters I had worked with in Milledgeville came here and started a farm. He had lost both of his sons in the war, and he and his wife wanted something small where they could make enough money to get by. They wanted to get away from anything that reminded them of their former life. With no children to inherit the farm, he left it to me in his will. He and his wife both died of pneumonia one winter, only three years after they'd moved here.

"When a hunter showed up on my doorstep in Savannah one day, I knew it was time to see the farm that was now in my name. I lived here for a few years until I heard that the priest had moved back to Europe."

We had reached the master bedroom by this point. I was happy to see that the furnishings here were a lot more in style with the house: the big bed with a carved head-board was already inviting me to curl up and sleep some more.

There were sheets in a closet, and I promised I would hang them outside in the morning to get rid of the musty smell. For now, though, they would do. Maxwell and I were both asleep within twenty minutes after arriving at the house. I didn't even take the time to undress.

I awoke the next morning with stiff arms and a runny nose. My sinuses were protesting the mix of smoke and stale sheets. Maxwell had gotten up earlier, and when I went downstairs, he was busy pushing open curtains and cracking windows open to get the air moving. It was cold outside, and there was a white layer of frost over the grass. It had been chilly in Savannah, but not cold. I had worn a light jacket to Grant's house, but discarded it once we got back to Shaun and Daisy's. That left me with nothing but stinky jeans and my Seekers tee.

I found the washing machine in the basement, threw my clothes in, and made a naked dash upstairs to the shower. There was no central heat in the house, and it would take time for the old radiators to warm up the drafty rooms.

When I had wearable clothes again, I took the sheets and towels and hung them from an old sagging clothesline outside. I figured the sunshine and fresh air would do more for them than the washing machine could. If it hadn't been for Maxwell's R8 sitting in the drive, I would have felt very old-fashioned. All I needed was a dress and an apron.

We were on the lookout for demon hunters all day, but there was nothing to disturb us. Maxwell stuck out in the grocery store with his suit, but I blended well enough. Maybe the people who eyed us would think that I was a local and he was my big-city boyfriend.

Three full days passed in complete peace. We made a run into Athens to get new clothes and toiletries, walked the old trails dotting Maxwell's property, worked on my self-defense training for hours, and occasionally checked in with Daisy and Carter.

In the evenings, Maxwell told me stories about his life

over the past several hundred years. He knew I didn't want to hear about his demonic conquests, so instead he told me about places he'd lived, customs throughout history, and people he had befriended. It was fascinating. When Maxwell talked about things like surviving an epidemic of the Black Plague, I wondered how he could ever be satisfied with his relatively quiet life now. Then again, I mused, maybe he welcomed the quieter life, without people dying horribly all around him.

Every time I felt complacency setting in, I reminded myself that we were still in hiding and an attack could come any day. By the time Friday morning rolled around—beginning day four of our strange country exile—it was easy to forget that we were supposed to be fearing for our lives.

"We can't stay here forever," I said over breakfast on Friday.

"Why not? We have everything we need." I tried to detect a hint of sarcasm in Maxwell's words, but I couldn't.

"I have a job that I'm supposed to be getting back to on Monday," I pointed out. Gosh, had I really only been off work for one week? My Christmas break sure hadn't turned out like I'd planned. "You have a business to run."

Maxwell waved a casual hand. "I can run my business from anywhere. If I need to be in a meeting in Savannah, it's a short commute for me."

"I think we'd both get bored out here. Neither one of us is suited to living in the sticks."

"Now that point is one I can't argue with. I do like a little excitement in my life." Maxwell smiled suddenly. "Maybe we could take up cow-tipping and square-dancing. Think I'd look good in cowboy boots?"

I laughed but didn't let Maxwell steer me away from the original subject. "We have to decide something," I insisted.

Maxwell reached across the table and squeezed my hand. "I know, but I'm not even sure it's safe for you to return to work. They could come after you there."

"But I don't want to stay here forever."

"It won't be forever. We don't need to make a decision right this minute, though. Let's talk it over for the next couple of days. By the end of the weekend, we'll know what we're going to do and where we're going to go."

As it turned out, we didn't have to wait that long before someone else made the decision for us.

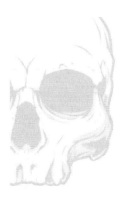

SEVENTEEN

Later that afternoon, I was playing a game of solitaire at the kitchen table when I heard the pop of Maxwell materializing near me. "How's it going with getting that TV and DVD player set up?" I asked, not looking up.

I heard the popping sound again, so I wasn't surprised that no one was there when I finally turned around. A moment later I heard the TV blaring from the living room. "Success!" Maxwell shouted.

I looked around me one more time, and an uneasy feeling crept over me. I called Maxwell's name as I walked down the hall toward him. "Did you just materialize in the kitchen?"

Maxwell didn't respond, but by the way his whole body suddenly tensed, I knew the answer was no. It was some other demon who had been in the kitchen with me, and that meant that someone had discovered where we were.

I wasn't entirely surprised, except for the fact that it was a demon and not a hunter.

Maxwell took my hand, and we walked as silently as possible to the kitchen. We never heard another popping sound, but we expected it every moment. My chest tightened, and my breaths came in shallow gasps. I had barely escaped the previous demon attack, and I knew they would be even more aggressive this time.

Still holding hands, Maxwell and I were practically back-to-back in the middle of the kitchen. The house was so silent that I could hear the ticking of the old clock in the living room.

We stood that way for at least twenty minutes, but functioning on the edge of panic can only last so long. Even knowing that something bad was coming, we both began to relax. My breathing returned to normal, and Maxwell's grip on my hand lessened.

Maxwell turned me around so we were facing each other. Just as he opened his mouth to speak, the doorbell rang. I jumped at the unexpected sound. "They're being terribly polite," Maxwell said. He pulled me with him to the front door: whatever happened, we would face it together. I instinctively knew that he didn't want me out of his sight.

We had just reached the front door when someone began to pound on the back door. Maxwell and I were unarmed, and I knew that we were surrounded, just as we had been at Shaun and Daisy's. We had been so foolish to come here, thinking that no one would eventually track us down. We should have continued moving, sleeping in a different bed every night.

Instead, we were trapped again. With only two of us to fight them, I doubted we would live through whatever was in store.

The person who had rung the doorbell was the same hunter who had fled from the nursery after he saw Maxwell's handiwork. I could see him through the leaded glass in the door, and he stared at Maxwell with wide, slightly manic eyes. My instincts shouted at me to run, to flee upstairs. The logical side of my brain protested that I'd be trapped up there.

At least we had a door separating us. That thought had

just crossed my mind when Maxwell reached forward and opened the door.

"I assume you were a friend of Joseph and Rob," Maxwell said cordially.

The hunter, already brandishing a consecrated knife, wavered. "Um, no, I never met them actually."

"What's your name?" I had no idea how Maxwell could speak so calmly.

"Arliss." The hunter looked suspicious now, like Maxwell was setting him up for a trap.

"Arliss, before you banish me to hell, let me tell you something about Joseph and Rob. One of them stabbed Betty, and the other shot her. I'm not sure you're avenging the good guys."

"They were fellow hunters. You are a spawn of hell," Arliss said firmly. "She must die, too, for killing a hunter to save a demon."

"That's not how it happened," I interjected. What the hell was I doing? We should be fighting back, or at least trying to escape. If we could just make it past whoever was still pounding on the back door, we could get to Maxwell's car. Instead, I found myself arguing my case. "Joseph was actually trying to drown me, and I fought back."

Arliss hesitated, but his resolve didn't lessen. "Then Joseph must have had some reason for it. I'm sure your association with this abomination led you to do something unholy."

"Oh, for the love of—" My words were cut short by a pop right behind me. I whirled around and saw a short, stocky man with dark hair and tan skin. He was one of the demons who had tried to kill me at The Hex.

"Hello, Betty," he said. Why was everyone being so polite? If there was going to be fighting and killing, then I was ready to get it over with.

The back door banged open with a loud crack: tired of knocking, our other guest had forced his way in. He appeared at the far end of the hallway, and I gave an involuntary groan. It was the hunter from Fort Pulaski. I briefly wished that we had left him inside Daisy and Shaun's house.

The demon turned around casually. "Perfect timing," he said.

I looked at the hunter while I pointed at the demon. "Could you banish him, please?"

The hunter barely looked at him. "I'm not after him."

The demon laughed, looking at me with mock pity. "Michael and I are old friends."

"I wouldn't go that far," the hunter growled.

The demon grabbed my arm and yanked me away from Maxwell. Michael stepped aside, letting the demon drag me down the hall even as I grabbed futilely at the walls to slow down our progress. I shouted as I fought against him, but he was too muscular. I was little more than an annoyance to him.

As the demon dragged me out the back door, I looked back to see Maxwell staring at me, oblivious to the hunters on either side of him.

I continued to struggle, and the demon finally threw me down onto the grass. He stood over me, his feet firmly planted on either side of my hips. "You are going to make me a very rich demon," he said, smiling.

"You might kill me, but I refuse to go to hell," I said. I had intended to sound brave when I spoke, but my voice was shaking.

The demon just laughed. "It's not your choice, Betty."

"I won't lose my faith because of you," I insisted. "I know how demons work. You prey on people until they lose their faith, until they curse God. You can't shake me."

My captor leaned over at the waist so that his face was just a few feet above mine. "That's really great. Congratulations. I don't care where you go after you die, as long as you die."

"Then you're not going to get much of a reward, are you?"

"There's no stipulation about where you end up. And if you're done arguing with me, then I'd like to be about my business." He leaned down further, arms outstretched.

I propped myself up on my elbows and began to scramble backwards, but the demon brought one foot down onto my chest. He pushed my back flat against the ground, and as the pressure increased, I felt my ribcage bow under his weight. I could barely get air into my lungs.

As I struggled to breathe, the demon crouched down and laid his hands on my shoulders. I knew what was coming, and soon the all-too-familiar warmth began spreading down my arms and into my chest. With only one demon trying to incinerate me, it was a much slower process.

I flailed and scratched my nails down the demon's arms, but he didn't relent. In desperation, I reached up and attacked his face with my nails. He deftly turned his head and bit down hard on two of my fingers. I howled in pain and returned to hitting and scratching his arms.

The burning inside my arms and chest increased, and I slowly lowered my hands to my sides. The pain made it impossible to concentrate, and as the heat grew, my energy diminished.

I heard feet pounding across the backyard, and I turned my head, hoping to see Maxwell running to my rescue. Instead, it was Michael. He stopped right in front of me, his face contorted in fury.

"Damn it, where did he go?" Michael had his quiver of arrows slung over his back, and for the first time I saw the bow in his hands. He also had a silver knife tucked into his belt.

Michael's question was directed at me, but I didn't know why he expected me to have the answer. I was too busy being killed to keep track of Maxwell's whereabouts.

"He's got to show up here at some point," Michael said. "He'll try to be a hero."

Great. I was going to die, *and* I was being used as bait to catch Maxwell. Again.

I wanted to shout at Michael, to ask him if he was really going to stand there and let the demon burn me from the inside out. I wanted to know if that was part of the holy mission he had undertaken. But I was drawing only enough air to stay conscious, and already my vision was tinged with a pale red as the demon continued to send scorching heat through me.

I was still mentally shouting at Michael when his mouth suddenly made an "O" of surprise and he fell forward, narrowly missing me. Maxwell was clinging to his back, and as soon as Michael hit the ground, Maxwell snatched an arrow out of Michael's quiver. Without hesitation, Maxwell plunged the arrow into Michael's back. The hunter's body spasmed with pain, then lay still. Maxwell had shoved the arrow into Michael's heart.

With the hunter dead, Maxwell launched himself at the demon, but there was a flash of black in my peripheral vision, and instead of flying forward into the demon, Maxwell's trajectory changed mid-air, and he fell to the ground behind me. All I saw was a figure in a black coat moving with him.

Despite everything going on around him, the demon still had me pinned to the ground, and he was still well on his way to killing me. I didn't know how long it would take Maxwell to dispatch the hunter he was currently fighting, and I determined again to act on my own.

If I could just reach Michael's knife, I thought, chancing a quick look at the dead body next to me. But no,

Michael had landed facedown, and I'd have to roll him over to get the knife out of his belt. Maybe I could reach an arrow.

Even as I tried to find an escape, a hand reached around the demon's neck and yanked him away from me. I didn't even wait to see the aftermath: I used all of my strength to sit up and heave against Michael's body so that I could grab his knife. He was too big for me to roll over, but I got him hoisted just enough that I could worm my hand under his broad stomach. My fingers found the bone handle, and I yanked as hard as I could.

I looked up, expecting to see the demon bearing down on me. Instead, I saw him engaged in a heated argument with someone, but at my angle, I couldn't see who it might be.

And then I heard the faint accent and knew it was Carlo. What he was doing here, or how he'd even found us, I didn't know.

Neither demon was watching me, and I slid the knife into the inside pocket of my jacket. It had been chilly in the house that morning, and I'd complained about having to wear my jacket indoors. Now I was grateful for the concealment it offered.

"What do you mean?" the demon was shouting at Carlo. "Of course you're out of line!"

"You still don't understand, do you?" Carlo spoke like he was trying to teach a very stubborn child. "You're setting a dangerous precedent for us all."

The demon laughed mockingly. "Yes, a dangerous precedent. It's just like a demon to do something outside the normal rules. In fact, it's what we're supposed to do. Think about what we're doing to their sense of right and wrong. Think of the promises, the sacrifice they're making."

"Think about what you're sacrificing!" Carlo was

173

shouting now, and his usually handsome face was contorted by his anger.

The demon's body crouched, as if he might spring at Carlo. Instead, he inched his way toward me, moving backwards so he wouldn't have to turn away from Carlo. "I know what I'm doing," the demon sneered. "And she's mine."

Finally, the demon chanced a glance back, realizing that I had moved. One hand darted out to grab me by my hair. I was about to bring the knife up when there was a loud crack, and the demon's hand suddenly began to burn. It was absolutely scorching heat, but it lasted only a fraction of a second. The demon disappeared, and I saw Carlo standing a few feet away, a gun in his hand.

The demon's clothes were lying in a heap on the ground. "You banished him," I said.

"Yes. It's horrible to have to take out my own kind." Carlo offered a hand to help me up. I took it cautiously, still unsure how trustworthy he was. He put the gun in the waistband of his pants instead of shooting me, so I decided to give him a chance.

Carlo pulled me to a standing position while I groaned loudly. Judging by the pain flaring through my chest, the demon had cracked a rib or two with his foot. Carlo seemed genuinely concerned, but I assured him I was fine.

"What are you doing here anyway?" My eyes roved all over the backyard for Maxwell, but there was no sign of him or the hunter who had tackled him.

"Keeping you safe," Carlo said casually.

"How did you find us?"

"The hunters found you. They followed you as far as a gas station when you left Savannah. They knew they couldn't follow you onto the back roads without being blatant about it, but at least it gave them an idea of where you might be going. They notified priests all over North

Georgia. They, in turn, notified their congregations." Carlo shook his head at me. "You two should have been more careful at the grocery store."

As angry as I was, I couldn't help but be impressed by the hunters' effective search methods. I doubted that the parishioners who had been on the lookout for us had any idea what Maxwell was or what the hunters were going to do to us.

Something still wasn't making sense to me, though. "The hunters are only going after Maxwell. Why didn't they help get this demon? He and that big hunter acted like they knew each other."

"Of course they do. They're working together. The hunters had once promised not to harm you. It seems they had some agreement with another hunter, who didn't think you deserved death."

I nodded. "Lou."

"The hunters did more than recruit ghosts to harm you. They also hired demons. They offered a reward for your death. Money, as well as immunity from the hunters for the next one-hundred years."

The reward had been offered by the hunters, not Satan. Suddenly I understood why the demon who had attacked me hadn't cared whether I went to hell or not. It really didn't matter where I went in the afterlife, as long as I went. It also explained why Carlo and the demon had been arguing.

"You told the demon he was setting a dangerous precedent," I said.

"Yes. Since the beginning, we have only ever worked for Satan. Taking contracts with other employers, especially those who oppose everything we do, is simply not done. For thousands of years, some of us have been given the privilege of wandering the earth, doing as we please. The only stipulation is that we fulfill our purpose. If one demon goes against the boss by working for hunters, the consequences could be severe for us all. We would be reined in with a tight hand."

"You weren't really trying to protect me, then. You were looking out for yourself." No wonder I hadn't been entirely trusting of Carlo. I could usually tell when someone wasn't being straight with me, and I hadn't been wrong to be wary of his kindness.

Carlo gazed at me for a long moment before he answered. "Yes and no. At first I was as excited as the other demons at the prospect of gaining immunity from the hunters. They approached me about allowing my ghosts to attack you. But you really are such a good soul. It was odd that the hunters—supposed men of God—could want someone like you dead. That line of thinking made me realize what a risk we were all taking. The lines between good and evil have blurred greatly because of you and Maxwell. Sometimes I'm not even sure which side is right anymore."

"Me, neither. Speaking of Maxwell, I hope he's okay. Do you know where he might have gone?"

I turned in a circle, looking at the woods around us and hoping for some sign of where Maxwell and the hunter had taken their fight. As soon as my back was to Carlo, he looped his hands inside my elbows and pulled my arms behind my back. I was so shocked that I didn't even raise my voice when I said, "Carlo, what are you doing? You're not working for the hunters."

"You're right. I'm not here to kill you, Betty. But your boyfriend has made my boss very angry, and he has to pay for his transgressions."

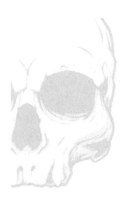

EIGHTEEN

I had never imagined that Carlo would want to banish Maxwell. Among the mix of expletives, exclamations of surprise, and protests that I shouted while Carlo forced me to sit down on the ground, I kept repeating one word over and over again: "Why?"

"It's like I said: we demons have been given our freedom in exchange for fulfilling our mandate from Satan. Every once in a while, a demon falls for a mortal. It's not unheard of, but Maxwell is legendary. For the demon who has sent some of the most promising souls to the fiery pit to be so consumed by a woman is extraordinary. How many people has he ruined since you two started dating? If the rumors are true, the only deaths on his hands were in defense of you."

"I don't understand why you need to banish him, though. Can't you settle for a stern lecture?"

Carlo barked a laugh. "Of course not. It wouldn't be effective. Keep your hands behind you, where I can see them. That's right." Carlo leaned down and waved his gun in front of my face. "I don't want to shoot you, but I will if I must. Anyway, what was I saying? Oh, yes. Maxwell must be banished to set an example. We can't have demons falling in love all over the place, neglecting their sworn duty."

"Maxwell and I have only been together for a few months. Considering that he's been around for hundreds of years, it seems like you could overlook this little incident." If Maxwell and I had to break up so he could continue to live, then so be it. I didn't like it, but it was vastly more palatable than seeing Maxwell banished.

"You've altered him forever, I'm afraid."

I didn't know what else to say in Maxwell's defense. Instead, I fell silent, listening hard for any sign that Maxwell and the hunter were nearby. After what seemed like an eternity, I saw Maxwell at the edge of the woods, walking from one of the trails we had taken a few days before. He moved slowly, limping slightly.

I stared hard at Maxwell, and when his eyes met mine, I projected every feeling of danger toward him. Judging by the resolve on his face, though, he already knew that he was walking into a trap.

Maxwell was unarmed, and I waited to hear the shot from Carlo's gun. When none came, I leaned back and peered up at him. The gun hung loosely from Carlo's fingers, and he slowly slid it into his waistband again.

A warning was on my lips when Maxwell got within six feet of us, but it was unnecessary. Carlo stated his intention before I could get one word out.

"Why?" was all Maxwell said in response.

Carlo gave Maxwell the same speech he had given me, adding, "If you're going to die for any mortal, though, I'm glad it's this one. I think she's actually worthy of it."

I shook my head. Since when did demons spout such chivalrous talk?

Maxwell looked at me, meeting my eyes with a calm gaze. "She is worth it, but I'd rather not go back to hell."

"I never expected you to go quietly." Carlo's voice was full of anticipation.

Maxwell slowly rolled up his sleeves. The cuffs were stained with blood. "Let's go, then."

Carlo needed no further prodding. He leaped at Maxwell, who immediately materialized elsewhere. Every time Carlo approached, Maxwell would disappear and show up in some other part of the yard. He was always in sight, but always too far for Carlo to reach him.

The strange game of cat-and-mouse only served to anger Carlo, whose countenance darkened with every narrow miss. He growled and stalked Maxwell like an animal, his eyes growing wild.

I sat unnoticed. Slowly, I began to ease myself backwards, hoping to get my back against an old well in the backyard. Staying out in the open like I was just seemed like a bad idea.

Maxwell materialized near the back porch, but this time Carlo didn't move. Ten feet separated the two, yet Carlo balled his hand into a fist as if he were going to throw a punch. Instead, he brought his arm back and made a throwing motion. There was a bright flash, and Maxwell was gone again.

When Maxwell appeared several yards to my right, Carlo threw again. This time I saw the bright ball of fire that erupted from Carlo's palm. It sailed right through the spot where Maxwell had been standing a split-second before.

Maxwell materialized on the other side of the lawn, and within seconds he had built up enough energy to create his own ball of fire. He released it just as Carlo threw his own, and both demons vanished as the fireballs broke apart and fell in embers to the ground.

I had never seen two demons fight each other before. They moved faster than I could have imagined, each materializing to throw a fireball, then disappearing just as quickly. They ranged all over the yard, eventually moving out of my sight into the front yard.

I was too afraid to follow them, and I bit my lip. What would happen if one of them hit the other? I doubted the fireball would do more than burn, but it could certainly be the distraction Carlo needed to subdue Maxwell.

Why didn't Carlo just use his gun? Were he and Maxwell fighting according to some kind of demon dueling code? If I had a weapon like that in my pocket, I would certainly make use of it.

Wait. I did have a weapon like that in my pocket. I'd been so distracted by Carlo's betrayal that I had totally forgotten about Michael's knife, still tucked inside my jacket pocket. The challenge would be getting close enough to Carlo to actually use it.

I stood slowly, wondering how I could even approach him when he was materializing from one place to another so swiftly.

The realization of what I had to do came to me as I began to walk toward the front of the house. It would be risky, for both Maxwell and me, but it was the best idea I could think of.

I edged around the porch, crouching low to keep out of sight. When I peeked out, I saw Carlo, his back to me, on the other side of the driveway. He disappeared just as Maxwell popped up, no more than ten feet from me.

"Maxwell! Materialize near me and—" I cut off my instructions abruptly as Carlo reappeared in the middle of the driveway.

I waited until I had a brief moment alone with Maxwell again. "Let Carlo get close," I said.

Maxwell didn't answer until he and Carlo had gone through another round of fireballs. "No," was all he said.

"Trust me." I hoped I had enough confidence in my

voice to convince Maxwell that this was the proper course of action.

After a few more minutes, Maxwell finally shouted, "Next time!"

I gripped the handle of the knife and steadied myself on the balls of my feet, ready to jump up when it was time. As promised, Maxwell materialized right in front of me, facing the front yard. I was still hidden by the edge of the porch, and I waited to see if Carlo would simply keep throwing fireballs or if he would approach Maxwell.

Neither of those things happened.

I heard Carlo materialize right behind me. I kept the knife low, hoping it was still hidden from him, as Maxwell turned around. "What now, Maxwell?" Carlo asked in an overly sweet voice. "I can kill her or I can banish you. If you dematerialize now, Betty will get shot before you can come back to rescue her. If you choose to defend her, then I'll shoot you. We've had some fun and let off a little steam, but I grow impatient."

I didn't wait for Maxwell's answer. I stood up, my back still to Carlo. "I love you," I said to Maxwell. As I spoke, I turned my eyes downward. Maxwell followed my gaze, and when he saw the knife, one corner of his mouth twitched with just a hint of a smile. His eyes, though, silently pleaded with me to be careful.

I turned around slowly. "This stops right now. I don't want to go through life knowing that Maxwell was banished to save me. You've said over and over that you don't want to hurt me, that you think I have a good soul. Believe me when I say that you banishing Maxwell would destroy me. I'd rather die than see that happen."

Carlo's lips narrowed into a thin line. "Betty, think about what you're saying. I really don't want to kill you. You'll be heartbroken for a while, but eventually you'll find someone else to love."

"I don't want someone else." As I spoke, I brought the knife up and shoved it as hard as I could into Carlo's chest, hoping I would hit his heart. I used both hands to push the blade in to the hilt.

Carlo's handsome face had an expression of sadness just before his body disappeared. I was left holding a bloody knife with a shirt hanging from its tip.

I fell back against Maxwell as I dropped the knife. I felt a strange mixture of elation and remorse. I had banished a demon, saving Maxwell in the process. At the same time, I had destroyed someone who had once saved my own life. It didn't seem fair for me to turn on Carlo like that.

Maxwell seemed to know exactly what was running through my head. "He would have killed you, Betty. And he wouldn't have felt nearly as bad about it as he made you think."

I turned around and wrapped my arms around Maxwell's waist. He slid his arms around my shoulders and squeezed.

"Ow," I said, wincing as my ribs protested. Maxwell loosened his grip, and I settled more comfortably against him. "Is everyone either dead or banished?" I mumbled against his collarbone.

"Yes. We're safe."

Maxwell and I both knew that it wasn't really over: every priest in the area had been alerted to us, and it was only a matter of time before someone spotted us and realized that we were both still very much alive. The bounty on Maxwell would go up, and more hunters would come after him. I realized that those kinds of risks were what Maxwell had been dealing with for centuries, but it was a new way of life for me.

At the moment, though, I didn't care. All I wanted was a hot bath and a long night's sleep.

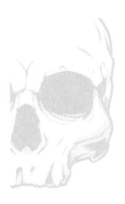

NINETEEN

The nightmares began that night. Banishing a demon didn't come without consequences, and many who dreamed of being hunters gave up after their first successful banishing. They just couldn't handle the nightmares that followed.

I woke up screaming in the middle of the night. I had dreamed of stabbing Carlo, only before he disappeared, he grabbed my arm and took me with him. I was instantly transported to hell with him, finding myself on a narrow island of rock, surrounded by a pit of fire. The flames lapped up my legs as I begged Carlo to save me. He only laughed harder the more I pleaded.

My legs were being scorched in the dream, and when I woke up, I could still feel the searing heat of the flames. I threw the covers back, expecting to see red, blistered skin.

I touched my legs cautiously, and in the moonlight I could see that my legs were, in fact, perfectly fine. My scream and my sudden movements had made my chest ache, though. I started to cry, but my ribs protested, and I had to take several deep breaths while I willed myself to remain calm. I lay back against Maxwell while he gently stroked my hair and made soothing noises.

"It was awful," I finally said.

"The dreams will fade in time," he assured me.

I sure hoped it would be a short time.

It took me an hour to fall back to sleep. I was so terrified of having another nightmare about Carlo that I was reluctant to let my mind relax, but I was still exhausted from the day's events, and I inevitably drifted off again.

In the morning, Maxwell rose quietly, allowing me to sleep in. I woke up sprawled in the middle of the bed, Mina curled up at my feet. Maxwell must have heard me stirring, because he appeared in the doorway with a cup of coffee for me. "Good morning," he said, sitting next to me and taking my hand.

"Morning."

"We said we would make a decision about what to do now."

I nodded. I wasn't sure I was awake enough to make any decisions.

"I think we should go home," Maxwell said.

"We don't exactly have a 'home' anymore," I said. "You can't go inside yours or mine."

"Then we'll find somewhere new to live. Together."

"Is it going to be safe for us?"

Maxwell didn't hold back. "No. It will never be safe for us. I'm going to have hunters after me until the end of time. Wherever I go, they'll eventually find me. I'd rather face them in the city I know and love than in some strange place. I think you're safe now. The hunters who wanted you dead are all dead themselves—most of them, at least —and the demons who were working for them aren't going to stick around with the losing team."

"I'm going to grow old, you know," I said abruptly. "You're going to look like this forever. I'm going to be thirty someday, then forty, then fifty…"

Maxwell smiled softly, his eyes sad. "You'll have found someone better than me by then. A mortal man. A good man whose past won't cause you pain."

"I don't think anyone could ever replace you."

"At any rate, you're not going to be an old lady anytime soon. Let's just take it one day at a time, okay? I, personally, am happy for every day I have with you, and for every day I don't have to fight for my existence."

"Okay." I drained my coffee cup and snuggled against Maxwell. We lay there for a long time, simply enjoying the peace and togetherness. I had thought that deciding where to go and what to do would be a huge task. I had pictured us going through one scenario after another, ranging from the exceedingly simple to the absolutely outrageous. Instead, it had been decided so easily. Going home to Savannah was the right choice. Our lives were there, my job was there, my mother was there.

And my friends were there. I knew that Daisy and Shaun would come back to Savannah, even though they would have to find a new home. And Carter, who came from a long line of proud Savannah residents, would never be able to stay away for long.

Later that afternoon, I called Daisy and Carter and informed them of our plans. Carter said that they had already returned. Kayce had a job she needed to get back to, and after her experiences with us, she was ready to get away from Carter and The Seekers forever. I couldn't blame her. We'd put her life in danger, and I was fine with her ignoring me if we ever ran into each other around town, as long as she never told anyone what we had been through together.

Carter offered to let all of us stay with him until we found new places to live. It was unusually polite for Carter, and I gladly thanked him for the favor.

At seven o'clock that night, Maxwell knocked on

Carter's front door. His home was one of the biggest town-houses I'd ever seen in the historic district, and it had been beautifully restored.

It wasn't Carter who answered, but Daisy. She embraced Maxwell and me, then pulled back and gave us each a hard look. I had a sinking feeling that she was harboring even more resentment about her house than I had anticipated. Instead, she said, "Something bad happened."

"What's wrong?" I asked, taking her hand.

"I mean something bad happened to you two. I can see it in your eyes."

"We lived through it, though," I assured her. "I didn't want to talk about it on the phone earlier. It will be easier to tell in person."

That was Daisy's cue to usher us in. I hugged Shaun and Carter before I settled gently onto a red velvet sofa. I was far too bedraggled to be sitting on such a posh antique. Daisy, always a good hostess, even if it was in someone else's house, had placed glasses of sweet tea in front of us within the first minute of our arrival.

"Where are Mick and Dwayne?" I was surprised that they weren't already handing mics to Maxwell and me.

"I sent them home. They'll be back to film future episodes of the show, but there's nothing going on right now for them to film." Carter shrugged, as if he was bored by the idea of life going back to normal.

Maxwell and I told every detail of our trip to Dewy Rose while Daisy interjected a lot of "bless your hearts." When we were done, she and Shaun expressed a great deal of satisfaction that we all seemed to be out of danger. Well, all of us that were mortal, at least. Maxwell was back to his usual level of danger, which he seemed perfectly capable of living with.

"Now we just need to find places to live," Shaun said.

"I thought we'd just live with Carter forever. His house is certainly big enough," I said.

"Actually, I can offer a solution," Maxwell spoke up. "Shaun, Daisy, you have no idea how sorry I am about your house. It's ultimately my fault. If I'd never introduced myself to Betty, we wouldn't be in this situation now. My townhouse is yours. It's paid for, it's big enough no matter how many kids you decide to have, and it's furnished. You'll have to convert a guest bedroom to a nursery, though."

Shaun and Daisy both began to protest, but Maxwell raised a hand. "All I ask is that you bring the baby out so I can see it. I won't be able to come visit since you'll be living on consecrated ground."

No matter how much Shaun and Daisy tried to reason with Maxwell, he wouldn't hear of it. Eventually, they graciously accepted, and within an hour, Daisy was already planning the first meal she would cook in Maxwell's spacious, modern kitchen.

If Daisy had been harboring any resentment toward me for the loss of her home, then it was certainly forgotten now. She and Shaun were still without many personal items, and Daisy especially mourned the loss of some heirloom jewelry of her grandmother's, but she assured me that she had cried over it enough, and she was ready to move on. "When our homeowner's insurance check comes in, you're going with me to the mall," she warned.

"Speaking of that, has anyone questioned what happened the night of the fire? I drove off in the most conspicuous getaway vehicle ever." I wondered if any of the neighbors had given statements to the police.

"It looks like we got really lucky there," Daisy said. "The house across the street from us is for sale, and the neighbors to either side were both visiting family for the holidays. If anybody further down the street saw anything, they aren't talking. I guess it's a perk of being well liked by your neighbors. When the police called to tell us about the fire, we feigned ignorance. Apparently the person who lives in the house behind ours is the one who called the fire department. They never saw any of us since we were in the front of the house at the time."

Daisy was right: we had gotten lucky. And since the police had verified that Daisy and Shaun weren't home when it happened, the bodies would probably never be discovered. Their ashes would just be shoveled away with the rest of the debris.

It was nice to know that something, at least, had gone right that night.

Dinner was nothing more than a few pizzas that we had delivered, but it was perfect. Carter constantly fretted about not spilling food on his rugs, reminding us that the one in the living room had cost more than what I made in a month. For once, he didn't annoy me. I just told Carter, "I promise I won't get a drop of sauce on your rug, but I can't promise that I won't spill any of my wine."

Carter responded by snatching up my wine glass and moving it to the kitchen. If I wanted to drink it, he informed me curtly, I'd have to drink it in there.

I knew I would have the nightmare again that night, but at least I went to bed with a mind at peace. My fear of Daisy's resentment had weighed more heavily on my mind than I had realized, and seeing her smiling at me and looking forward to moving into her new house put me at ease.

The next two weeks passed with relative harmony. Living with Carter was a challenge sometimes, and I had to keep Mina confined to the guest bedroom we occupied because of Carter's eternal fear for the safety of his rugs, but otherwise things were pleasant. I was actually happy to be back at work. The mundane tasks I did in the marketing department at Coastal Health Hospital took on a fresh new feel, and every day I was grateful for the normalcy of it all.

Daisy and Shaun moved into Maxwell's house with ease, since they really had nothing to move. Their biggest task was to pack up Maxwell's clothes and personal belongings, and I came over to help with that after work each day.

Maxwell spent his time looking for somewhere new for us to live. I went to my apartment every few days to pick up fresh clothes, though every time I approached the front door, I threw a cautious glance behind me, afraid I would find a demon hunter there. Each evening, Maxwell would show me pictures and details of every place he thought looked like a possible choice for us. My only stipulation had been that it must be in Savannah's historic district.

On the second Saturday since our return from Dewy Rose, Maxwell and I headed out to look at a townhouse that showed a lot of promise. Actually, two of the other houses we had looked at were fine by my standards. In fact, they were above and beyond what I had anticipated moving into. I had been thinking of getting a little apartment somewhere, but Maxwell figured he might as well buy a new townhouse.

"It's a lot older than my previous townhouse, but judging by the pictures, it's been meticulously restored," Maxwell said over breakfast. It was the first house we'd discussed that he really sounded excited about.

"We need to head out soon if we're meeting the realtor at ten," I said, glancing at the clock. "Carter, what are you up to today?"

Carter looked sulky as he answered. "Putting together the nursery." Daisy worked for Carter's father, and he had taken up a collection for her from everyone in the law firm. Instead of giving her the cash, though, Mr. Lansford had purchased an entire nursery with it. It was far nicer than what Shaun and Daisy could have afforded on their own.

"Cheer up. A little hard labor will be good for you. Maybe you'll actually break a sweat."

Carter grimaced and mumbled something about paying someone to do it for him.

Maxwell and I walked to the house we were going to look at. It was south of my carriage house apartment and within walking distance of the Burglar Bar. I liked the idea of the house being close to my current residence, but not too close.

The townhouse was just off of Troup Square, and as soon as we rounded the corner and I saw the "For Sale" sign on the front porch railing, I actually squealed with delight. I had thought I had outgrown that years ago, but apparently not. Maxwell, who had already walked by the house, turned his eyes to me, soaking in my reaction. "You like it?"

"I love it. We should probably look at the inside before we take it, though," I said, winking. The realtor was already there, thank goodness, because we were both anxious to see if the interior was as perfect as the exterior.

The house had a ground-level basement, and the front steps led to a set of double front doors with stained glass windows. The ornate wrought iron railings looked more like something from the French Quarter in New Orleans than a piece of Savannah architecture. The façade was pale stucco with accents of Savannah gray brick around the windows on all three stories.

The realtor could sense our anticipation, and she wisely remained quiet after she unlocked the front door and waved us in. The house spoke for itself. The hardwood floors, the crown molding along the ceiling of each room, the bright dining room with wainscoting: it was like my dream home. I had always wanted a historic home in the heart of Savannah, and I had considered my carriage house as the first stop on the way. To go from my tiny apartment to this lavish townhouse, though, was a bigger leap than I had imagined.

The house was perfect. Maxwell and I barely discussed whether or not it was the one we wanted. I warned him that I would only be able to pitch in a fraction of what the mortgage would surely cost, but Maxwell insisted it was fine. "I'll be living here long after you're gone," he whispered, "so I ought to pay the bulk of it."

Other than that unwelcome reminder that Maxwell would still be in the prime of his life after I was in the grave, I couldn't have been happier. I had Maxwell, a new home to look forward to, a baby shower to plan for my best friend, and no one trying to kill me.

After Maxwell wrapped things up with the realtor, we walked away feeling optimistic. We didn't anticipate anything cropping up to keep us from closing on the house. Instead of heading back to Carter's house, Maxwell turned onto Habersham. "I know it's early, but we need a celebratory drink at The Burglar Bar," he said.

I couldn't have agreed more.

We only walked one block before my perfect day took a terrible turn for the worse. As we stood waiting for the traffic light to change at East Liberty, several women who were clearly tourists turned to me. "Can you please help us? We're trying to find the cemetery," one of them said.

"Of course," I answered. I pointed Colonial Park Cemetery out on their map. "You're really close to it. Just go straight to East Oglethorpe, turn left, and you'll be at the front gate."

They all thanked me, but my response died on my lips.

I looked up and realized that a man standing on the curb near the tourists had turned to stare at me. It was Lou.

When my eyes met Lou's, his eyes widened in panic. Without looking, he ran into the street, never seeing the white van speeding toward him.

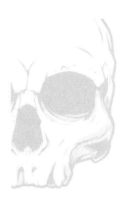

TWENTY

Everything happened at once, and I never moved from my spot. There was the sound of a horn, the squeal of tires, and the screams of the tourists in front of me. One of the women fell over backwards as someone landed on top of her.

Then there was an awful, awful thud as the van made contact.

I instinctively shut my eyes, and when I opened them, I saw a body lying awkwardly in the middle of the intersection. There wasn't much blood, but the angles of the legs and arms were unnatural.

It was Maxwell.

I covered my mouth to prevent the scream that began to bubble up and ran forward. Already people were rushing toward him to help. I passed the women and saw Lou in their midst. He was the one who had landed on one of them. Maxwell, I realized, had materialized in the road to push Lou out of the way.

There was blood pouring from a cut in Maxwell's scalp, and I dropped to my knees next to him. He was unconscious, but his chest still rose and fell. Tears welled up in my eyes as my hands hovered over him. I didn't know where to touch him because he seemed to be injured everywhere.

"Maxwell," I said, putting my face close to his.

"Are you with him, ma'am?" a man asked.

"Yes, he's my boyfriend. We're buying a house." Tentatively, I put my fingers against Maxwell's cheek. There was no response.

"It's okay," the man's voice said again. "An ambulance is on the way."

My tears dried instantly at those words. "No, he doesn't need one," I said. "He'll be fine." Of course, I reminded myself, Maxwell is a demon. He heals. By the end of the weekend, it will be like nothing had ever happened to him. Why was I being so silly? I'd seen Maxwell shot before, and he'd gone right home afterward and taken a shower.

The man didn't answer me. He just patted my shoulder sympathetically. "It's true," I told him. "Lou can tell you how fast Maxwell heals." I pointed my chin in Lou's direction, but he was gone. I looked at the growing crowd around me. The onlookers pushed closer, inching toward us, until the ambulance forced its way through. Instead of helping the man who had just saved his life, Lou had fled.

Two EMTs came over, and with only a precursory nod to me, they began inspecting Maxwell's body. "He'll be fine," I told them.

"Ma'am, we're taking him to Coastal Health. You can get an update on him there." The female EMT gave me a brief but sympathetic look. "We'll get him to the ER immediately."

"No, he just needs to go home and rest," I insisted.

But the EMTs didn't listen to me. They got him on a stretcher and were rolling Maxwell toward the ambulance as I continued to tell them that it was all unnecessary. When Maxwell was secured inside the ambulance, the female EMT turned to me and put a gentle hand on my arm. "Do you have someone who can drive you to the hospital?"

I wasn't going to win this battle. "Yes. I'll call my friend to take me."

As I pulled out my cell phone to call Daisy, I heard the woman say to her partner, "Girl's in shock."

"No," I mumbled behind her back. "He's a demon, and you're all going to call him a miracle when he walks out of the hospital tomorrow."

Daisy was shocked at my news but, like me, she was well aware of Maxwell's healing capabilities. She promised to pick me up within ten minutes. While I waited, the same trio of tourists who had asked for directions approached. They offered to help, and I welcomed their company while I waited for Daisy. Even though I knew that Maxwell was going to be okay, it still rattled me to see him so very beat up. I'd never seen him unconscious before, either, and it gave him a strange air of vulnerability.

Daisy did even better than promised, arriving in just over five minutes. She eyed the front of the van with apprehension. "He must be terribly injured," she said.

"He'll be fine," I said for what felt like the millionth time.

At the hospital, we were forced to sit in the waiting room for over two hours. I grew more and more anxious to see Maxwell, but every time I inquired, I was told that the doctors were still tending to him. I tried to take it in stride: if Maxwell was being helped along with his healing, then it couldn't do any harm.

I was pacing back and forth in front of a window when a nurse came out and called my name. I rushed up to her. "Yes? I'm Betty Boorman."

"Come on back, honey." The nurse led us down several halls, and when we reached Maxwell's room, she stopped and turned to me. Something in her face made me afraid, and I reached back and grasped Daisy's hand. "He's pretty beat up," the nurse said. "And he's got some head trauma, so he's in a medically-induced coma right now. The doctor can tell you more."

The nurse nodded at someone behind me, and I turned to see a doctor approaching us. I wanted to see Maxwell immediately, but the doctor wanted me to be prepared first. "He's got a long list of injuries," the doctor said. "His shoulder was dislocated when he was brought in, and we reset it. He has a broken tibia and fibula, a cracked ankle, broken ribs, and we put twenty stitches in his scalp. Because he was unconscious when he arrived, and because he hit his head on the pavement, we're keeping him sedated and monitoring his brain for any swelling. All of his other injuries will heal completely. The head is the critical thing right now, but I'm optimistic that he'll be just fine."

That list was nothing for a demon. I thanked the doctor and entered the room with Daisy, expecting to see Maxwell sitting up in bed and lamenting having to wear a hospital gown instead of a tailored suit.

What I saw instead shocked me into silence. "He's still unconscious," I said.

"Betty, the doctor said they're keeping him sedated." Daisy squeezed my hand reassuringly.

"Right." Still, Maxwell looked awful. There was a huge chunk of his hair missing. It had been shaved off to accommodate the stitches in his scalp. His face was sallow, and his normally high, elegant cheekbones now looked gaunt. An oxygen mask obscured much of Maxwell's face, and an IV in his arm was attached to two plastic bags filled with clear liquid. There was a cast on his leg, and Maxwell's arms were dotted with abrasions. What frightened me most was the sheer helplessness that I saw before me.

I walked forward slowly, as if I might disturb Maxwell or do further harm to him. I patted his hair awkwardly, then grasped his immobile hand. At least I can hold his hand because it's not injured, I thought. Bruises were forming on Maxwell's arms, deep and purple. Something as simple as a bruise should have healed already.

I don't know how I wound up in the chair next to the bed. Daisy must have led me there after I started crying. Eventually, she brought me a cup of coffee from the cafeteria. "It won't be as good as what Carter has at his house," she said, "but it will make you feel better."

As the hours passed, I continued to sit there, waiting for any sign that Maxwell was healing. When a nurse came in for a routine check, she commented on Maxwell's high fever.

"No, he's just naturally warm," I told her.

"I've had plenty of patients whose temperature ran higher than average, but a hundred and three is a fever," she said.

I just nodded my head as if I saw her point.

Shaun came to relieve Daisy that night, sending her home to sleep in a real bed. I insisted on staying, still waiting for a sign that Maxwell was healing. I barely slept that night, contorted in my chair with a blanket and a pillow.

The next morning, there was still no change in Maxwell's appearance. All I wanted was for him to open his eyes and tell me that he was okay, but he didn't.

Carter took a turn keeping me company, and he sat in the chair next to me the entire time he was there, holding my hand with real concern.

Even my mom came to sit with me, despite her lingering reservations about Maxwell.

On Sunday night, Mom went home when it got well past her bedtime. Shaun was on the way, and I didn't mind having a few solitary moments. I sat with my feet tucked under me, staring at a book that I wasn't really reading.

When the door to Maxwell's room opened, I didn't

look up. I waited for Shaun to sit down next to me, but when he didn't, I looked up. It was Lou.

I put down my book and got up, moving to stand over Maxwell. "He saved your life," I said.

Lou just nodded.

"Please don't do this." I felt tears already slipping from my eyes. Maxwell was unable to move, let alone defend himself, and it broke my heart to think that Lou would take advantage of him this way. I didn't want to fight Lou, but if he tried to banish Maxwell, then I would do whatever I had to.

Lou stared at Maxwell, closely examining him from head to toe. Lou leaned in close so that his face was only inches from Maxwell's. He squinted, his brow furrowed, as if he was concentrating really hard.

"So it is true," Lou said under his breath. He straightened up and locked his eyes onto mine. There was no remorse in them, no apology. He simply said, "God bless you, Betty." Without another word, Lou turned and left.

I was still standing over Maxwell's bed when Shaun came in. He hadn't seen Lou and was just as curious as I was about the strange encounter. I could only shrug my shoulders and rejoice that Lou hadn't banished Maxwell right there in the hospital.

Sometime during the night, I roused when the nurse came by on her rounds. She gave me a hopeful smile. "His fever has broken," she said.

"That's impossible." I got up and put the back of my hand against Maxwell's forehead. It was cool, no different than my own skin. I touched his arm next. It was the same. I didn't know what was happening to Maxwell, but if he wasn't hot to the touch, then something must be wrong. He wasn't healing, and now his very life force seemed to be draining away.

I articulated my fears to the nurse, and she assured me

that Maxwell was, in fact, healing. The doctor hoped to ease him off the medication that was keeping him sedated now that Maxwell's head was less of a concern.

Early the next morning, after I had called work to explain why I wouldn't be there (it was ironic since I worked in the admin building of that very hospital), the doctor came in and repeated the nurse's optimism. "We'll take him off the medication today. He could wake up as early as this afternoon, but he'll be groggy," he said.

Groggy was better than unconscious, and I spent the entire day looking for any signs of movement or awareness in Maxwell.

Daisy showed up in the afternoon with a change of clothes for me. "Carter says he had to scoop Mina's litter box. I think he actually hired someone to come in and do it for him, though," Daisy said.

I smiled, the first time I'd done so since just before Maxwell's accident. I was still smiling when I glanced at Maxwell and saw that he was smiling back at me.

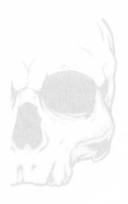

TWENTY-ONE

Maxwell took a while to really wake up. He kept drifting off for long periods of time. Still, he was waking up, and I had finally seen his blue eyes after three days of waiting. It was enough hope to give me the patience I needed.

I squeezed Maxwell's hand when he opened his eyes again later that night. His oxygen mask had been removed, and he began to speak after taking a long drink of water. "I am so glad to see you," he said. Maxwell's voice was low and raspy, but just hearing it brought tears to my eyes.

"I'm glad to see you. I've been so worried."

"What day is it?"

"It's Monday night. You've been unconscious since Saturday morning."

Maxwell stretched and winced. "I hurt." He looked down at his body. "Is that a cast?"

"Yes. You broke your leg and cracked some bones in your ankle. Also, you got stitches in your head." I decided to save the rest of Maxwell's injuries for a later conversation. I didn't want to overwhelm him.

Maxwell slowly soaked in the information. He stared up at the ceiling, looked earnestly at me, then hesitantly raised his arms to examine them. Finally, he took my hand and began running his fingers over my skin. "How do I feel?" he asked.

"I imagine you feel pretty bad, but you're a better judge of that than me."

"No, I mean, how do I feel to you? What's my skin like?"

"Your temperature is really low. You had a fever, but you still felt like you normally do, and then the nurse said the fever had broken. Ever since then you've felt no different than me."

Maxwell closed his eyes. He brought my hand to his lips, and when he looked at me again, one tear slid down his cheek.

I felt panic tighten my chest. "What does it mean?"

"It means that I feel no different than you because I am no different than you. I'd heard rumors about this, but I didn't know it could actually happen."

"Are you dying?" I asked. Now I was crying, too. Behind me, I heard Daisy gasp.

"No, not any faster than you are, at least." Maxwell smiled. "I'm mortal, Betty."

I blinked, the words not sinking in. "But you're a demon."

"Not anymore. I'm human now." Maxwell began to cough then, as if he was offering proof of his imperfect mortality. He drank more water, then said, "Every demon has heard the legends about others who turned mortal. I had thought it was impossible."

I was about to ask how when the nurse bustled in. "Oh, you're awake, Mr. Damon. Welcome back. Your girlfriend has not left your side, and I know she's glad to see you're back with us." Waiting for her to finish checking out Maxwell was agonizing. She finally left, promising that a doctor would be in to see him soon.

As soon as the door closed behind the nurse, I simply said, "How?"

"I made a selfless sacrifice. After the way Lou gave up

your friendship and turned against you, you had no sympathy left for him. I certainly had none. But I saved him, anyway. I didn't even think about it. I just saw someone who was in need, and I acted. I've never done that before."

"The only way to not be a demon is to do something a demon would never do," I said.

Maxwell nodded and smiled in response. "I've been given a choice. I have a life to live now, and how I live it determines whether or not I go back to hell when I die."

"That means you're going to grow old," I teased.

"Will you still love me when I have gray hair?"

"Of course."

Maxwell sighed and his eyelids fluttered. He was exhausted from our short conversation, but before he drifted off to sleep, Maxwell whispered, "Sweet dreams, Betty."

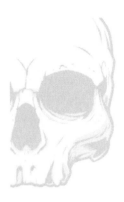

EPILOGUE

"Do you have your socks? What about your bowtie? You packed those cufflinks, right?"

Maxwell gestured at the garment bag in his hand. "Betty, you've made me double and triple check everything. I promise you, it's all in here." He laughed and squeezed my hand with his free one. "You weren't even this nervous at our own wedding."

"I know. It's just that it's Carter, and he's so picky about everything. If his Best Man doesn't look perfect, then he'll be complaining about it for the next ten years."

"If I look perfect, then I'll look better than the groom himself."

"You already look better than Carter," I said. "I'm glad he found himself a nice rich girl that we actually like."

"You just like her because she enjoys going on investigations with us."

"It certainly doesn't hurt. All right, I've got to run upstairs and get showered. I'll see you at the church. Daisy and I will be sitting together. Oh, and don't let Shaun do that weird thing with his hair. It's not trendy; it's dorky." I kissed Maxwell goodbye and saw him out, stepping outside to soak in the beautiful Savannah sunshine. Mina followed me and sat serenely at my feet. It was nearing fall, which meant Halloween and the usual increase in calls from people wanting help from The Seekers.

It also meant that Shaun and Daisy's wedding anniversary was approaching, and I had already promised to babysit Shaun Maxwell Tanner while they went to dinner. He was a toddler now, and I'd be chasing him all over the house.

I smiled at some tourists who were ambling past on the sidewalk below before retreating through the double front doors. As I walked up the stairs, I mentally reviewed my wardrobe. Even though I wasn't in the wedding, I knew Carter would expect me, as well as every attendee, to be spectacularly dressed. It was, after all, being hailed as the social event of the year. And knowing Carter, he had probably invited a few members of the media to cover it.

I didn't mind. Maxwell had made sure that news of his mortality got spread to priests and demon hunters, so there was no one left for us to hide from. Besides, I had figured prominently in Carter's last book, and I secretly enjoyed the ensuing notoriety.

I was just about to step into the shower when my cell phone rang. I was surprised to see Carter's name on the caller I.D. He was getting married in three hours. What could he possibly need to speak to me about?

"Hey, Carter," I answered. "You getting cold feet?"

"Yes. I'm getting cold everything. You wouldn't believe the cold spots in this church. The preacher says he once saw a hymnal fly across the sanctuary, too."

"That's impressive."

"Yeah. Keep your calendar open for three Saturdays from now. I'll be back from my honeymoon by then, and I promised the preacher that The Seekers would investigate."

"Yes, sir. Now go get married!" I hung up the phone and grinned at myself in the mirror. My eye caught the sticky note that had once hung on my computer monitor at work. It now lived on my side of the bathroom mirror, where I could see it every day. "Get awesome life," it read.

There was a big check mark next to the words.

THE END

A NOTE FROM THE AUTHOR

Thank you for reading *Ghost of a Hope*! I hope you have enjoyed being a part of Betty's world. *Ghost of a Threat* was the first novel I ever wrote, and these characters will always have a special place in my heart. Reviews are one of the best ways a reader can support indie authors, so would you please leave a review for this book? Your support is appreciated!

Thank you,

Beth

ACKNOWLEDGMENTS

Thank you, readers, for coming on this adventure with me. I hope you have enjoyed getting to know Betty, Maxwell, and the rest of the gang as much as I have. I owe a debt of gratitude to my mom Ann for her editing skills, my husband Ed for his support, and my friend Kristine for being such an enthusiastic test reader.

WANT MORE?

SWEET DREAMS

ETERNAL REST BED AND BREAKFAST
BOOK ONE

A Paranormal Cozy Mystery Series
Set in the Betty Boo, Ghost Hunter World

Emily Buchanan has always dealt with ghosts at Eternal Rest Bed and Breakfast—after all, it is next to the town's historic cemetery. When paranormal activity begins to escalate, though, she knows that someone—or something—is desperately trying to communicate. When a body is discovered in a shallow grave at the cemetery, an old town scandal is resurrected, and Emily knows she has to find out what happened if her guests and her ghosts are ever going to get a good night's sleep.

BOOKS BY BETH DOLGNER

The Betty Boo, Ghost Hunter Series
Romantic Urban Fantasy
Ghost of a Threat
Ghost of a Whisper
Ghost of a Memory
Ghost of a Hope

The Nightmare, Arizona Series
Paranormal Cozy Mystery
Homicide at the Haunted House
Drowning at the Diner
Slaying at the Saloon

The Eternal Rest Bed and Breakfast Series
Paranormal Cozy Mystery
Sweet Dreams
Late Checkout
Picture Perfect
Scenic Views
Breakfast Included
Groups Welcome
Quiet Nights

Manifest
Young Adult Steampunk

A Talent for Death
Young Adult Urban Fantasy

Nonfiction
Georgia Spirits and Specters
Everyday Voodoo

ABOUT THE AUTHOR

Beth Dolgner writes paranormal fiction and nonfiction. Her interest in things that go bump in the night really took off on a trip to Savannah, Georgia, so it's fitting that the Betty Boo, Ghost Hunter paranormal romance series takes place in that spooky city. Beth's first book was the nonfiction *Georgia Spirits and Specters*, which is a collection of Georgia ghost stories.

Since Georgia is obviously on her mind, you might think Beth lives there. Well, she did, but these days she and her husband, Ed, live in Tucson, Arizona, with their three cats. Their Victorian bungalow is a lot smaller than Eternal Rest Bed and Breakfast, but Beth likes to think it's haunted, even though Ed swears it's just drafts.

Beth also enjoys giving presentations on Victorian death and mourning traditions as well as Victorian Spiritualism. She has been a volunteer at an historic cemetery, a ghost tour guide and a paranormal investigator.

Keep up with Beth and sign up for her newsletter at BethDolgner.com.

Made in United States
North Haven, CT
16 October 2023

42812551R00133